FAMILY DUEL

Pearl Shandon is the offspring of a first, rash marriage, and because her father is aware of her likeness to her dead mother, their love for each other is always clouded by distrust. Most of Pearl's youth is spent with an aunt but when the aunt dies and Pearl goes to live with her step-mother and half-sister, disaster overtakes the family. For this, Pearl's father believes her to be responsible.

The question posed in this perceptive story is whether this beautiful, enigmatic girl is a monster of iniquity or cruelly misunderstood.

FAMILY DUEL

Hebe Elsna

COLLINS
8 Grafton Street, London W1

William Collins Sons and Co. Ltd
London · Glasgow · Sydney · Auckland
Toronto · Johannesburg

ISBN 0 00 233244 2

First published 1954
This reprint 1987

© Hebe Elsna, 1954
Originally published by Robert Hale
© This revised edition, Hebe Elsna, 1979

Made and Printed in Great Britain
by William Collins Sons and Co. Ltd, Glasgow

✳ CHAPTER 1 ✳

Pearl Shandon had been awake for some hours when she heard the postman's knock. She listened to his retreating footsteps and then got out of bed. Nobody else in the bungalow stirred, and Pearl put on her dressing-gown, slipped her feet into soft-soled bedroom slippers and went down the long passage.

Kate, her step-mother, prided herself on the perfection of Sunaglow, and had furnished it in what she believed to be the height of taste and luxury. It was certainly comfortable, though certain aspects were apt to set Pearl's teeth on edge.

The floors were thickly carpeted throughout, and Pearl's footsteps were noiseless. It was almost without a sound that she picked up the letters and extracted the newspapers which had been pushed partly through the letterflap. Three papers this morning instead of one. It was a special occasion and Rose had made it plain that the production deserved it.

Pearl was rather surprised at that. Throughout the last week Rose had been nonchalant over the production of David's play at the local theatre, and Pearl had thought it tactful to conceal her far greater interest. Yet surely her sister must have felt some pride when it was announced that David was the winner of the hundred pounds prize given by the local theatre for the best three-act play entry by an amateur. Well, if she had, she revealed very little. She had shown only doubt and alarm. It must have been daunting for David, Pearl reflected.

With the papers and letters in her hand, Pearl went into the dining-room; a large and pleasant room with long windows which opened upon the garden and gave a vista of the sea beyond. The bungalow was built in an exposed position on the cliffs, and during the three months of Pearl's stay there, the wind had often moaned and raged for hours on end. To her that was desolate and depressing, but neither her half-sister nor her step-mother appeared to be affected

5

by it. Kate would build up a huge fire, and say cosily that it was a wild night, and Rose would cheerfully agree. Both of them approved Brightwell and everything it had to offer.

Pearl went across to the windows and pulled back the glazed chintz curtains, where the bright and brittle sunshine of an April morning shone into the room, and she reflected with relief that although there might be stormy days to come, the winter at least was over.

It was odd that she should be in such a critical mood that morning, for when she had arrived in January, sad and lonely in her bereavement, she had been appreciative of the homely welcome extended to her.

Probably it was a sign that her unusual nervous condition had mended, and one day not so far distant, she would be ready to return to London and to all her friends there. But when she did, it would be at her own wish and at her own will.

As that thought crossed her mind, her face involuntarily hardened. It was never a softly feminine face, though both Kate and Rose considered her gentle and adaptable, and frequently said so. Pearl's beauty was of the classic type; straight nose; full, curved mouth, deep-set eyes, large and dark and long. Her honey-coloured skin was smooth, a shade or two darker than her long, fair hair, which was brushed back from her broad forehead. Later, when she was dressed, she would plait it around her head, a style which suited her.

Now, realizing that it would not be long before the rest of the household would be stirring, Pearl with a casual glance through the letters to discover if any of those amongst them were for her, which they were not, put them down on the sideboard and turned her attention to the newspapers.

She spread one out on the centre dining-table, found that for which she sought on the third page, and smiled with pleasure at the headlines :

SUCCESS OF PRIZE WINNING PLAY AT THE ARTS THEATRE

She went on to read the long paragraph which was laudatory in the extreme, and finishing that, turned to the second

6

paper, in which the notice of the new play achieved equal prominence. So absorbed was she that she was unaware of her sister's entrance, until Rose was actually at her elbow. Then she looked up to smile at her, noticing with surprise that Rose was dressed and had evidently been out.

'I thought you were still asleep,' said Pearl.

Rose shook out a wet towel and a swimming-suit. 'I woke up early and the sun was streaming in. When I looked out of the window, I saw there were a few people in the sea, so I decided I might as well join them, and have my first swim of the year.'

'Courageous of you. It must have been terribly cold.'

Actually Rose's face was pale, and her teeth were chattering, but she said : 'It wasn't too bad, though I could do with a warm now. Isn't that lazy girl up yet?'

'You forget. Norah's been given a week's holiday.'

'How tiresome. Mummy is too soft with the people we employ. I suppose I'd better rake out the ashes and get a fire going.'

Pearl said rather absently : 'Leave it, it'll do as it is.' But Rose, paying no attention, bustled about producing sticks, re-filling the coal scuttle. 'So the papers came. Are the notices good?' she asked, as the paper and sticks kindled.

'Excellent.'

'Read them out,' Rose suggested. 'Now where in the world has that girl put the cruet?'

Pearl's brows drew together in a frown. She disliked the way in which the Shandons spoke of those they employed. Suppressing her irritation, Pearl said : 'They're too long, and the story of the play is all mixed up with the criticism of it. Here, read for yourself.'

Rose, now busy setting the breakfast table, took the paper held out to her. Her eyebrows lifted slightly at the sight of the spreading headlines, but she showed no other sign of excitement. Pearl was aware of an unreasonable annoyance.

'Why, this is quite good,' said Rose at last, and with surprise.

'Yes. Didn't you expect good notices?'

'I didn't think much about it, one way or the other. It

would have to be a very bad play to get slated.'

'But it wasn't a bad play,' said Pearl in her gentle but decisive voice.

Rose smiled indulgently: 'This all seems more important to you than it does to us. It's because you've spent years mixed up with theatre people.'

Pearl said nothing. By this time she was accustomed to Rose's patronizing attitude towards the world of the theatre. It was a profession which was scarcely proper, and those who followed it were suspect. Pearl's Aunt Cynthia had often said that her brother Miles had never reconciled himself to the fact that she had been sufficiently talented to earn a great deal of money through acting.

Suddenly, as Pearl read the description of the play in the third paper, she laughed. 'This,' she said, 'is the best notice of the lot, but the reviewer describes David's speech, and says he was petrified with terror.'

Rose also laughed. 'So he was. He told me afterwards that he wouldn't go through such an ordeal again for ten times the prize money. I'm glad he feels that way.'

'Why?' Pearl set aside the paper to look at her sister.

Rose was warm now, and the blue tinge had vanished from her face, which was a pretty one. As she and Pearl were but half-sisters it was not surprising that they had little resemblance to each other. Rose was small and plump, whereas Pearl was tall and slender. Rose had curly brown hair, sparkling blue eyes and a retroussé nose. Her mouth was sweet, though her chin was obstinate. On one cheek there was a scar; a straight white line, but not sufficiently deep or noticeable to be really disfiguring. Of the blemish, Pearl was more conscious than Rose – guiltily conscious.

'Well, it's been fun for him, but it wouldn't do to lose his sense of proportion,' Rose explained, 'to look upon play-writing as his life-work, just because he won the prize offered by a small, provincial theatre.'

'It's a beginning,' Pearl submitted.

'I'd rather think it was an end.'

'You would?'

'Yes, it's distracting. All very well as a hobby. Men need hobbies, but David got so het-up about it, and he kept dashing away to rehearsals when he was needed at the factory.

His father and Daddy were very decent about it, but it couldn't go on. Now I hope he'll calm down. The play will run for two or three weeks and that will be the end of it.'

Although Pearl had realized that this would be Rose's point of view, she had not before heard it put forward so definitely. Anger stirred in her, though her calm face betrayed no sign of it. It was, she told herself, a purely disinterested anger, for David Page was nothing to her. She had seen little of him during her three months' stay at Brightwell for when he was not working at the factory, the family business which it was presumed he would eventually inherit, he and Rose were seldom apart.

'It might get to London, and to the West End.'

Rose stared at Pearl, and then she laughed: 'Of course it won't.'

'But it's an exciting play and original – there's a lot of thought in it.'

'I suppose that's true, though for myself I prefer a more straightforward sort of play. But to get a London production is out of the question. David would need to have important friends and interest, and he has neither.'

Pearl shook her head in disagreement: 'It doesn't follow, but even if it did – I know a few people.'

'Mostly has-beens; you said that yourself. Aunt Cynthia was famous once, but she was ill and out of it all for ages. She hadn't been on the stage for several years and must have lost touch.'

'Not altogether.'

Rose said with decision: 'It would be fatal for David to get ideas about himself.'

'He's very modest.'

'And I hope he stays that way.'

Although Rose was smiling and spoken evenly, Pearl suspected hostility, but if that existed it was of short duration, for the younger girl moved nearer to her and said: 'Pearl darling, you're a lovely person. You know I think so. But you don't really understand us here.'

'Don't I?'

Pearl smiled, because Rose's arm was about her waist, because the pretty face was being rubbed in a kittenish fashion

9

against her shoulder. It occurred to her that in some ways Rose did resemble a kitten. She had endearing ways but then, too, she had sharp claws which she would not hesitate to use if necessary. She could fly into violent tempers if frustrated.

'You think I don't want David to get on,' said Rose, 'but I'm really ambitious for him. I'd do anything to help him with his real work.'

'You mean at the factory; learning how to pile up money?'

'Money is not to be despised, but it's not only that. A family business is something of which one can be proud. The Shandons and the Pages have been in partnership for over a hundred years. David will carry it on, and when we marry and have children, then our eldest son will take his place in years to come. I feel proud and happy when I think of it. It's a kind of immortality.'

'I see that,' Pearl agreed.

'For a time,' Rose continued earnestly, 'both Daddy and Mr Page were worried about David. When he left college he wasn't a bit interested in the factory. It was as though he wasn't interested in anything. He had to start from the bottom; that's part of the tradition. But he dawdled, had no enthusiasm until . . .'

'Until he met you?'

'Well, of course he had always known me. He didn't just meet me.'

'In a way he did. After you had been in France and Germany for two years, learning the languages, and then returned here to teach, you must have seemed very different.'

'I suppose so,' Rose agreed.

'But only superficially different,' Pearl reflected. Miles and Kate Shandon had done their utmost for Rose, had given her the best education in their power. She had been bright at school, and had decided that languages were her forte. She had begged to be allowed to study abroad and to take her degree later, which would be an easy matter once she was proficient in French and German. To that her parents had agreed, but after all Rose had not entered the University as a student, for soon after she returned, she had struck up a fervent friendship with David Page, and it had been evident that although she was ready and eager to teach, that would be only for a few years. To marry David had become her goal.

Pearl said : 'The scar had faded, was scarcely noticeable by the time you were grown-up. David must have been surprised to find you such a pretty girl.'

Rose laughed : 'Well, pretty or not he fell in love with me. It made a big difference. David began to take an interest then and to work – he knew he would have to, if we were to marry and have a home of our own. Of course,' added Rose with unexpected candour, 'I put the idea into his head, but then I expect girls generally do when a man is sort of dreamy and quotes poetry to them and never seems to think it's necessary to save a penny. I do believe David would have stayed romantically in love with me for years, and never done a thing about it.'

But that, Pearl reflected, was only because David was not nearly so deeply in love as he or Rose imagined. Not that it mattered, for in all probability neither of them would discover it for themselves.

'I was glad when I heard of it,' Pearl said soberly. 'I was nursing Aunt Cynthia at the time, and life was grim, but when I knew you were in love and engaged, I no longer felt so guilty about you.'

Astonishment flickered across Rose's face, and her hand went up to touch her scarred cheek : 'Because of this,' she exclaimed. 'But it was only a children's quarrel and I was equally to blame.'

'You didn't throw a knife at me.'

'No – a lamp and I missed you.' Rose laughed.

Little she realized even now, thought Pearl, what an entire change in her life had come about through the half-forgotten quarrel. All the blame had descended upon the older sister, and the pain and horror which Pearl had seen then on Miles's face would never be forgotten by her. Kate, naturally, had been shocked, frightened, angry; but these reactions had been normal. Miles, Pearl now realized had taken an abnormal, exaggerated view of the same thing, and that was because – because . . .

Her thoughts broke off as she usually forced them to break off when they dwelt upon her father, and she said: 'I never forgot it.'

'Nor did I,' said Rose. 'Being rushed off to hospital and having a fuss made over me, and nobody bothering about the broken lamp, and then after a day or two to come home and find you had been sent away to Aunt Cynthia. It wasn't fair on you.'

It had been grossly unfair, an injustice which Pearl had never forgiven, and yet, in some ways, she had been happier with Cynthia Shandon than she could have been had she lived with Miles and his second wife and her young half-sister.

Pearl had loved and admired Cynthia. No doubt she had been brought up in a ridiculous way, for she had been in Cynthia's confidence when she was no more than a child. She had known all about her triumphs and her disappointments, about her casual love affairs. Cynthia had hidden nothing from her and had explained little. Later, when Pearl had grown from a child into a beautiful young woman, her aunt had been surprised because she held men at a distance. She had expected her to marry early or at least to have love affairs but Pearl, though much admired and easily friendly, had been remote.

Cynthia had given her a good life until illness had stricken her down. She had earned a great deal of money for many years and nothing was too much for Pearl, who had had expensive clothes, holidays abroad, all the amusement she could possibly require. Cynthia had loved her and been proud of her. Had she been her mother she could scarcely have loved her more.

'She was very good to me,' Pearl said, her expression softening.

Sometimes Rose speculated about Pearl's life which had been so unlike her own; coaxed her to talk of it. It must have been exciting, she supposed; first nights and dinner-parties and mingling with famous people, but all that had been brought to an abrupt end when Cynthia had been stricken with paralysis. Then it must have been as though prison doors had closed on Pearl.

'You must have had dreadful years with the poor soul,' she

said. 'It was a shame, for although you and I fought, we were fond of each other. There were Daddy and Mummy too – you must have missed them.'

'Father came to see us sometimes,' Pearl reminded her.

'But he couldn't often manage it. Were you dreadfully alone?'

'Oh, no. Aunt Cynthia had many friends, and she still liked to see them, even when – even when . . .'

Pearl set her lips tightly, remembering those last months; so pitiful, so hopeless, with Cynthia scarcely able to talk or to move; but she had been brave, heartbreakingly brave.

'I'm sorry I spoke of it. I'd like to think you could forget it,' said Rose remorsefully. 'Anyway, it's all over now.'

As though such years could be ever really over or really forgotten. It would have been different had she cared less for Cynthia, or if she had really cared for many others. But there were so few.

Pearl was aware that she loved infrequently. Rose was different. She would have said now and believed it that she loved Pearl and that Pearl loved her, after three months of reunion, but her elder sister would have smiled at such a facile affection.

'Yes – it's over now,' she assented.

❋ CHAPTER 2 ❋

Kate Shandon, in the big, comfortable bedroom which she shared with her husband, was putting the finishing touches to her morning toilet. In the bathroom which was her especial pride, for at the turn of the century few except really important houses could boast of one, she heard Miles splashing. They had both of them had a late night, and in consequence neither of them had risen early. If Norah had not been on holiday she would have brought Kate a cup of tea, and she would have felt less sleepy.

Really they were stop-at-homes, she reflected placidly. That came of living at Brightwell. When they had the Northpond house it had been otherwise; then they were

13

always on the go; parties and whist-drives and the theatre. Kate had enjoyed it all, but that had been chiefly because with Rose away, first in Germany and then in France, she had been lonely. Once the Brightwell bungalow was built, it was different. For one thing Miles was a bit later getting home and she had more to do for Norah, the maid they now had – though honest and reliable – couldn't cook, so that meant there was the evening meal to get. But Rose, teaching in the district, was company. Sometimes she would go out with David, but mother and daughter had a lot in common. For the last few months there had been Pearl to consider.

When Cynthia Shandon died, and Miles and Kate went to London for her funeral, Kate had insisted they must bring Pearl home with them. For some reason or other, Miles hadn't seemed too keen, but Kate was shocked by Pearl's appearance – such a lovely girl and so tired and thin and nervy. She had had a hard time, no doubt about it.

Miles said that Pearl would be unlikely to settle down in a quiet place, that she had friends and interests which were very different from theirs. But Kate, while agreeing that this was true, had said it wouldn't hurt her to have a quiet holiday, and that she need not stay a day after she had had enough of them. It was gratifying now to realize that Pearl as yet showed no sign of tiring either of her family or of Brightwell. It did Kate's heart good, and she often said so, to see the friendship which Rose had struck up with her half-sister.

As for Pearl herself, no one could be easier. It had been a pleasant surprise to Kate to discover that her step-daughter was domesticated, really more domesticated than Rose. She could cook well and she liked a place to be spotless. With all her gentle, high-bred ways, which Kate openly admired, she was not above working hard around the place, and never was a girl more easily pleased. Sometimes Kate thought she was a bit too quiet and self-contained, but then of course poor Cynthia's death was so recent.

Kate smiled as the low murmur of voices reached her. Evidently Pearl and Rose were up and chattering away nineteen to the dozen. That was Rose all over, standing about with not a thing done towards getting breakfast.

Starting towards the door, Kate called to Miles in the

14

bathroom: 'You won't be much longer, will you, dear?'

'Five minutes. I've got to shave,' her husband answered.

'Be as quick as you can. We're late.'

Pearl and Rose looked round as Kate came in, and both wished her good morning. Rose went to her and kissed her; their deep affection expressed itself more demonstratively than was usual; but as Kate sometimes reflected with satisfaction, her Rose was the cuddly kind. She liked you to kiss her and to make a fuss of her.

'I overslept.' Kate smiled upon both girls. 'Why didn't you wake me?'

'It's Saturday, Mummy. No reason why you shouldn't lie in for once.'

'I suppose it doesn't much matter,' Kate conceded, 'though there's always plenty to do. It was a good party last evening. Did you enjoy it, Pearl? You were rather quiet.'

Pearl thought of the noisy, congratulatory party held at a hotel in Northpond. The theatre people had been nice, she thought, pleased for David, and taking little credit to themselves for the smoothness of the first night performance. Knowing nothing of provincial repertory theatres, Pearl had been surprised by the all-round capability of the cast. The man who played the leading part was as good as any actor she had seen in London.

'I was in a kind of dream,' she explained. 'David's play still held me. I couldn't forget it.'

Kate, puzzled, shook her head. 'So fantastic. I couldn't grasp half of it. Queer how David thought up such things. I see you have the papers. Are the notices good?'

This last was addressed to Rose, who answered: 'Nothing but praise.'

'Oh well, they would of course be kind to a local writer,' said Kate comfortably.

'But the notices are not a bit condescending,' Pearl protested.

'Oh no, dear, I'm sure they wouldn't be. Miss Anders on *The Sun* is such a nice woman. She writes herself, on the woman's page; a weekly article called *Look for the Sunshine*. She finds a verse of poetry to fit each piece, it must be quite a job. I saw her at the theatre last night, and said I did hope she would find something kind to say about David's play, and she said it was her duty to be kind to beginners as they were so easily discouraged. A really nice woman – there's no professional haughtiness about her.'

'But Mrs Shandon, you can't compare her work with David's play!'

'Of course not, but David hasn't to earn his living by writing,' Kate returned, and then before Pearl could explain that that was not at all what she intended to convey, she added : 'Pearl dear, do you have to call me Mrs Shandon? Couldn't you make it "Mummy" as Rose does?'

Pearl moved slightly away from her, turned so that her face could not be seen. There was a faint edge of chilliness to her voice as she replied : 'I'll try to remember to say Kate. It would be too bad if people thought you had a daughter of my age.'

'You're not much more than two years older than Rose; though it's true I wasn't twenty-one when she was born,' said Kate.

Rose laughed and squeezed her mother's plump waist. She looked at her lovingly. Mum was grand, thought Rose, and she did look young with her unlined pink and white cheeks, her bright eyes and glossy brown hair; but she was also a bit of a goose. Rose said teasingly : 'Last time you were twenty-three.'

'It's not really so young,' Pearl said. 'My mother was only seventeen when she died.'

What had made her say that? She regretted the words as soon as they were uttered, but for a moment it had been as though the room was darkened, as though that darkness was the expression of her pain and anger. Both Kate and Rose were startled, for it was the first time they had heard Pearl speak of her mother, as why should she, since the poor thing had died when she was born? After an uncomfortable silence, Kate said :

'Yes, it was very sad,' and then quickly, bent on changing the subject, she moved from Rose's encircling arm and said : 'Just look at the time! I must see about breakfast. Pearl, hadn't you better get dressed? The bathroom's empty now. Your Dad has had his bath. Rose, what made you go out so early?'

The last was an afterthought, for it had only just occurred

16

to her that her daughter was wearing her top-coat, and Rose answered in an offhand manner. 'I went for a swim.'

At that, Kate glanced at her with disapproval. She said: 'No wonder you look peaky. It's too early in the year. Really, you worry me. You know how you got cramp on that cold day last summer. Only that your Dad was with you, I don't know how you would have got back to the shore.'

'I should have managed. It wasn't that bad, and it was only the once. I'd never had cramp before. Anyway, I'm quite warm now.'

Kate hesitated, wanting to say more, but doubtful if it would be wise. Rose was a good girl, but she could be headstrong, and she resented interference in her ways. As though, thought Kate, you could prevent yourself from interfering when you were a mother, especially when you found it hard to realize that your only child was a grown woman.

Rose, as though to prove how warm she was, took off her top-coat and threw it on a chair. As she did so the chain she was wearing round her neck slid to the ground and lay there in a tiny coil of brightness.

'There now,' her mother reproved, 'you might have lost that outdoors and never seen it again. I told you the other day the clasp was a bit bent.'

Rose stooped to pick up the chain, and rising became aware of Pearl's intent and interested gaze. 'It's only my old charm,' said Rose, 'but I don't believe I've worn it since you came home.'

'I've not noticed it if you have,' replied Pearl. 'May I look at it?'

'Of course.'

The chain and the small oval disc which was attached to it slid into Pearl's palm, and she bent over it, examining it closely. 'This,' she said, 'must be very old. Has it been in your family for a long time? Is it a sort of heirloom?'

Kate laughed. She said: 'I wouldn't say we go in for heirlooms as a family, and certainly not for heathenish things of that kind. But Rose likes it. You might think it was a valuable jewel; she's even worn it going to a really big dance, you'd have expected her to prefer the turquoise pendant her Dad and I gave her on her twenty-first.'

'I don't see why I shouldn't value it, though of course not

17

in the same way,' said Rose defensively. 'That and my engagement ring are the only good pieces I have.'

'Maybe on your wedding day you'll get a brooch to match the pendant,' said Kate fondly.

'Where did you get this?' Pearl asked.

Rose explained that she had seen the disc in Paris on her homeward journey more than a year ago. 'It was in a queer old shop, on a tray with a lot of other bits and pieces. Somehow I couldn't take my eyes off it.'

Pearl turned the disc over in her hand. She said : 'It seems to be a charm.'

'For good luck, do you mean?'

Pearl shook her head doubtfully : 'I don't know, but I shouldn't want to part with it if it were mine.'

'Neither do I,' said Rose, 'so it's of no use you putting your eye on it. What do you make out the figure to be?'

'It's a man – a god of some kind, enclosed in a pentagram.'

'A pentagram? Isn't that a magic symbol?'

'A mystic one – Greek or Egyptian, I'm not sure. There's lettering, but it's too blurred to be legible.'

'Daddy and I made out that the figure was carrying a torch in one hand and a shaft in the other,' Rose supplied.

Pearl, with a mounting interest, was remembering all she had read about magic and mystic symbols. During her aunt's last illness, her reading had been extensive, and she had made quite a study of witchcraft and magic. Most of it was nonsense, but nevertheless she had come upon strange incidents for which it was difficult to find a rational explanation. Now, out of this wealth of lore which she had accumulated, memory came back to her, and she said with certainty : 'This is meant to represent the sun god. It must be centuries old and it's made of bronze.'

'I knew that of course,' said Rose. 'I wouldn't have been likely to get anything valuable for the little I paid, but the chain is gold. I bought that later, so that I could wear the pendant. It's not pretty or showy, but people are always curious about it, when they notice it. The clasp is not safe, as Mum says, and I shall have to take it to a shop and have it straightened out.' As she spoke, she held out her hand for the bauble and Pearl reluctantly surrendered it.

Kate, moving towards the kitchen, spoke with mild impatience : 'Do hang up your coat, Rose. Your Dad will be along in a minute and wanting his breakfast; Pearl, if you hurry, you'll have time to get dressed while I'm cooking it. At this rate the day will be half over before we've made a start.'

✳ CHAPTER 3 ✳

Miles Shandon looked forward to the weekends; they were part of his compensation for living in Brightwell instead of Northpond.

In his opinion the drawbacks were many, and the daily journey by bus was the most obvious of them, though lately he had played with the revolutionary idea of trying out one of the new horseless carriages. They weren't all that reliable, however, though Miles had a shrewd idea that it would soon be almost commonplace to own one. Mercifully, neither Kate nor Rose were showily ambitious. Money in the bank : that was the ideal for the Shandon family, as it was for most of their friends. If you were born to high-up notions that was all right, but if not, they were to be shunned and scorned.

It was a good principle, Miles thought, and often congratulated himself because he had married a sensible woman to whom thrift was second nature. Of late years he had talked her out of some of her economical habits, but she came of a slightly lower rank of life, and had a horror of what she called 'uppishness'. She had even doubted the wisdom of Rose's education abroad, thinking it might give her notions above her station.

Miles, leisurely shaving, smiled as he remembered this. Kate need not have feared for Rose, who was a level-headed girl, sensibly resolved to earn her own living until the time came for her to marry David.

The smile broadened as Miles remembered the fur coat which he had bought Kate for Christmas. The first she had ever had. It was a good coat; a sealskin, rich and heavy, which would last a lifetime. Kate had been awed, and her inclination was to hang it up in her wardrobe on a padded hanger with moth balls dangling from it in a small, ornamental bag. But Miles insisted that she was to wear the coat through the winter, whenever she went out, and very handsome she looked in it. Both he and Rose had been proud of her. Kate had been glad of the coat, too, when they went to London for poor Cynthia's funeral in the coldest month of the year.

Miles's smile merged into a frown. Queer that with all her docility, Kate could sometimes stand out for what she considered right. He hadn't wanted her to bring Pearl back to Brightwell, but she had insisted, had been shocked when he said his elder daughter had many friends who would be delighted to give her house room. It was Pearl's right, Kate insisted, to be with her own people and she had refused to consider anything else. Well, he supposed it had been natural. Pearl, poor child, had looked ill enough. She had been pathetically sad and listless, and had clung to them both. His beautiful Pearl – there wasn't a day in his life he was unconscious of his pride in her; of his doubt, his foreboding.

He knew so little about her – he knew so much. Now that she had been part of his daily life for three months, she was still an enigma to him. She was a clever girl who had been well educated and had read deeply. When she chose, she could talk with authority on many subjects, but unless lured into such conversations she was inclined to be silent; a good listener. Miles had little idea of what went on in her mind, and realized that he would be safer not to know. The expressionless love which existed between them was a tortured emotion, and he ignored it as much as possible.

Surprised that Pearl had settled down and was on such good terms with Kate and Rose, he secretly regretted it. Her presence here was a complication, and Miles, who was more selfish and more lazy-minded than he realized, disliked complications.

He was vaguely aware of Pearl's resentment, her silent criticism of him, and there would have been none of that had she lived on in London, and he had occasionally seen her there. Then such visits would have been a welcome break and a delight to him. As it was, he was too conscious of playing a deceitful part, too conscious of undercurrents, the existence of which were undreamed of by Kate or Rose.

Disturbed and irritated by these unwelcome reflections, he finished dressing and went along the passage to the living-room, to find his women-folk present, but no sign of the breakfast which in the ordinary way would have been over an hour ago.

Rose bade him good morning. Pearl glanced at him, but said nothing. She was not even dressed for the day, Miles noticed, but she was beautiful with her long, thick rope of fair hair, and her white house-coat moulded to her graceful form.

Kate exclaimed with vexation as she saw her husband glance round the room. 'We're late,' she apologized, 'but I'll soon get the breakfast going, that is if these two girls will stop chattering and give me a hand. Mrs Doyle has stopped coming. She says her family need her, and Norah won't be back from her holiday until Tuesday.'

Miles said: 'You could do with a maid to live in. I've told you so before.'

'Oh, no!' Kate was emphatic. 'There's little enough work to do in a modern place, and I'm hale and hearty, thank God.'

'It would look well though,' Rose suggested. 'Somebody to answer the bell and to be here when we had visitors.'

That was the kind of remark warranted to arouse Kate's disapproval, and she said sharply: 'Now Rose, I can't do with that sort of nonsense. There's no need for outside show, not in this family. Everyone knows we're in a good position, and that the only reason you teach, and I do part of my own housework, is because we'd be miserable if we were idle.'

Not too pleased at being thus openly reproved, Rose shrugged. 'It wouldn't be outside show, it would be a convenience. As for teaching, I don't see any reason to apologize for that. It would be wrong to waste my education. Of course it will be different when I'm married; then I shall give it up. Looking after David will be a full time job.'

Kate, her brief annoyance forgotten, smiled fondly at her. She said: 'It certainly will, especially when the babies start to come along. Pearl dear, do wake up. Is anything the matter?'

Pearl started as though she had indeed been roused from a dream, and Rose said: 'I showed her my old pendant, Daddy, and it so fascinated her that she stared and stared at it. It's not the first time I've seen people look a bit queer when they've handled it.'

'Perhaps they realized they were holding light and truth,' Pearl said, and her eyes rested dreamily upon her sister.

It was the strange, inscrutable look which antagonized Miles, which he distrusted, could not understand, and therefore feared. He had seen it in Pearl's eyes more than once. It was as though she stood away from them all and viewed them objectively. 'What on earth do you mean?' he demanded.

Rose explained: 'Pearl says it's a charm and very old. She thinks the figure is the sun god. She's green with envy because it's mine, not hers.'

Pearl's smile flickered over them both, but her voice was serious: 'Yes, I am,' she said.

'Because you think it's lucky?' Rose examined the bronze disc with interest. 'Then I shall certainly hang on to it.'

'It mightn't be lucky to you; only to some people.'

'You won't persuade me to give it to you. You have no end of jewellery, you greedy thing. Lovely stuff.'

Greedy was the right word, thought Miles, watching Pearl's face, hearing the lightness of her voice.

'Shall I trade with you?' she suggested. 'The sapphire bracelet which you like so much.'

Really startled now, Rose gazed back at her. Pearl couldn't be serious – but she was. 'Good gracious! That's valuable.'

'Yes – well . . .!' Pearl shrugged that away as of no concern.

It wasn't important to her, thought Rose. When Aunt Cynthia was alive, she had given Pearl beautiful things, and when she died everything had become hers. Was it quite fair? Although Rose had scarcely known her, she also had been Cynthia Shandon's niece.

After a moment of irresolution, Rose shook her head and dropped both chain and charm into her skirt pocket. 'No,' she said, 'I'll keep it.'

22

'Very well.' With a gesture which sketched indifference, Pearl moved towards the door, and something prompted Rose to say : 'I'll leave it to you in my Will.'

'Thanks.' Pearl's laugh floated back as she went down the passage to her room.

For a moment Rose's expression was speculative, and then she said : 'It's queer that when anyone wants anything you have, it makes you hold on to it.'

Miles who was still unaccountably ruffled, said with impatience : 'Superstitious nonsense! If there's to be bad feeling between you, you had far better throw the thing away.'

Rose opened her eyes very wide : 'Bad feeling between Pearl and me! There couldn't be. She's a lovely person.'

Miles's murmur might have been one of assent. He picked up a paper, discovered the notice of David's play and started to read it.

'Everyone admires her,' Rose persisted. 'People say – your beautiful sister, and do bring your interesting sister round to tea, and surely your sister will join the tennis club, and so on. There's something exotic about her which fascinates them, and although she has such a quiet manner there's something about that too.'

In some ways, Miles thought, Rose was very young for her age. There was a simplicity about her, a clarity of purpose. She was cleverer than her mother, and she had the advantage of a better education; but she greatly resembled her. Both of them had the same type of one-track mind. He said with an effort : 'Do people know that Pearl's mother was a foreigner?'

'Some may,' Rose answered indifferently. 'Mum and I don't talk about it, and they'd be unlikely to question Pearl. For all she's so gentle, she knows how to freeze people.'

'She has dignity,' Miles agreed.

'Yes – quite the grand manner. I can imagine how she would look in a mantilla, slowly waving a huge fan to and fro, while she watched one of those horrible bull fights without a quiver.'

'Don't let your fancies run away with you,' Miles advised.

'No – I mustn't. If I said anything like that to Pearl, she would laugh at me.'

Miles picked up the paper again and spoke with his eyes still

23

on the printed page. 'I'm glad she's making friends, but it must be dull for her here, and I doubt if she'll want to stay for long.'

'But she says she's never been so happy, and Mummy and I love having her,' Rose protested.

'That's good.'

A mutinous expression crossed Rose's face. She wished Miles would put down the paper he was reading or pretending to read, and come out into the open; wished he would discuss the matter reasonably.

'Daddy, you're so queer about Pearl,' she complained. 'She's your daughter as much as I am. Aren't you fond of her?'

'That's a ridiculous question.'

'Well, I suppose you must be, but you're not exactly warm to her.'

Miles sighed but gave her his attention. He made an attempt to explain that which could never be explained to Rose or to her mother. 'Pearl,' he said, 'has lived away from us for many years, and sometimes I find it difficult.'

'I don't see why you should, if she doesn't. I always feel upset when I think how she was sent away in disgrace, just because she and I had a fight. We can't even remember what it was about.'

'Does that matter? Pearl was better off with Cynthia who understood her and was very fond of her.'

'But she can't have had much of a time these last years with Aunt Cynthia so hopelessly ill. Mum and I think it's been dreadfully hard on her, and that it was more than time she came home.'

'You are both blessed with forgiving natures,' Miles drily observed.

He vividly remembered that long-ago scene, if Rose did not. Pearl, white of face and unrepentant; Rose screaming with hysteria and blood pouring from her cheek; Kate in a frenzy she might be marred for life. He had known guilt and horror and a hideous sense of responsibility. It had seemed as though the beautiful elder child, whom in spite of all misgivings he loved, had turned into a small, frozen fiend.

'Oh Daddy, don't look like that,' cried Rose. 'It's too silly. You can't think I still bear Pearl a grudge, because of this.'

Her hand went up to the faint scar on her cheek, of which for years she had scarcely been aware. Her voice was incredulous.

'Some might,' said Miles.

'But it was only a squabble between kids. It just happened that Pearl threw straight.'

'Yes – a knife,' her father grimly reminded her.

'Is that any worse than a lamp?'

'No, no worse,' Miles admitted, and when he looked back upon the incident in a detached and reasonable way, he realized why, to Rose, he seemed absurd. How could he explain to her that it was Pearl's expression which had been so unnatural and so long to be remembered. A cold, still rage; a deep, unchildish enmity; something that was almost pleasure.

To his relief Kate at the moment appeared at the kitchen door, and looked at her daughter with a comical despair. 'Rose dear,' she appealed, 'do for goodness' sake set the table for me. I can't leave this fry for long enough.'

'Sorry, mummy.' Rose was affectionately remorseful. 'But really – here's Daddy as good as saying that Pearl ought to be a perpetual outcast because we had that quarrel when she was twelve and I was two years younger.'

Kate looked from father to daughter with indulgent tolerance. 'Such nonsense!' she said. 'And the scar hardly shows at all now.'

'It hasn't spoilt anything for me,' said Rose. 'It hasn't made any difference. It didn't stop David from wanting me.'

'I should think not indeed,' said Kate, as she returned to the kitchen with Rose following her.

✳ CHAPTER 4 ✳

In her bedroom Pearl was dressing with mechanical speed; a cold sponge-down in lieu of a bath; a hair-brush wielded vigorously; a dust of powder and her long locks twisted about her head. She took a plain brown wool dress from her wardrobe and put it on.

Pearl's room was impeccably neat, and in an indefinable way reflected her personality. There were her favourite books between alabaster book-ends, and a small clock which was also of alabaster. Her brushes were of ivory with her initials in gold. A fine linen cloth which she was embroidering for Kate was neatly folded on a side-table.

Rose, who was casually untidy, admired Pearl for her sense of order, but confessed that she could never emulate it.

It was a spacious room furnished in oak with a good deal of pink about it in the way of cushions and runners and eider-down, and this, of course, was Kate's taste. Pearl's room in her London home was furnished and decorated in cream, with-out relief. Both Rose and Kate would have been astonished by its restrained luxury. But Pearl had settled down at Brightwell, as though such surroundings were customary.

Actually externals mattered little to her, though Cynthia's aim had been to surround her with luxury. Pearl liked to be solitary, quiet, orderly, and although she had often craved for a view other than that afforded by her London bedroom which looked out upon a narrow, uninspiring garden, she had never said so. At Brightwell, the vista from her window was certainly an improvement, for she had the cliffs and the sand-dunes and the limitless expanse of the sea.

She stood now looking out of the window, and her ex-pression told little of her thoughts, though she was brooding on Rose's bronze disc and on Miles's irritation.

He had mistaken her, of course, had thought that she attached some superstitious importance to the thing, which was not so. She had coveted it for its age, for the sense of history, of ancient mystery. Centuries old, the thing must be, and what stories it could tell if it were possible to strip back the veil of the past; shocking stories possibly, which if they were revealed to Rose would make her shudder and fling the thing away from her; but Pearl would have prized it the more for a sinister history.

Her thoughts had taken her far away from her surround-ings, but she was brought back to them as she heard Rose's voice calling her. 'Pearl! Pea-rl! Breakfast is ready.'

Pearl turned from the window and called back: 'I'll be

along in a minute.'

She was still wearing her low-heeled bedroom slippers, but she kicked them off, and looked round for the brown shoes which matched her dress.

Rose busied herself between the kitchen and the living-room, bringing in china and cutlery, setting the table for four, and talking to Miles as she did so. His responses were sparse. Rose, he thought, lacked tact, badgering a man with questions before breakfast, especially when they were unwelcome questions about his elder daughter.

'It's just that you have a bee in your bonnet, about her,' said Rose.

'For the Lord's sake don't use such absurd expressions,' he retorted.

'Yes, well I know it is silly,' Rose conceded. 'Clichés are a bad habit, and I must cure myself of using them. What I meant to say is that you can't possibly be jealous of Pearl's mother, can you now?'

It did then occur to Miles that unless he contrived to infuse more cordiality into his manner, he might be constantly subjected to such remarks, and he said with half-humorous reproof : 'My dear child, if you can suspect that, the insect to which you refer must be firmly lodged in your own headgear.'

Rose laughed : 'Well, I did agree it was silly, and doesn't mean a thing . . . but then so many of those sayings mean nothing; gilt on the ginger-bread, and a needle in the hay-stack and heaps of others.'

Miles put down his paper : 'The notices of David's play are good,' he said. 'Let's hope he doesn't allow this writing craze to interfere with his work at the factory.'

'Oh, he won't do that,' said Rose positively. 'He's thrilled because you and his father said you would make him a junior partner next year, when we marry. We've decided to build, Daddy.'

'You have?'

'Yes, a small house farther along the cliff; as like this as possible. There are so many things to plan – the furniture and the colour scheme and everything; and then the wedding itself. I'd like to have a white one, but no bridesmaids except Pearl.'

'You can't count on her being here as long as that,' said Miles, and getting up he went to the sideboard and examined the letters which he had only just noticed. There was nothing of importance. A bill or two, a circular, three receipts. Miles wished there had been some important communication in which he could have become absorbed.

'Why shouldn't she be?' Rose said. 'I tell you, Daddy, she's content, she's happy.' And then as her father received this in unresponsive silence, she sighed, saying: 'I don't understand you. I simply don't.'

Kate caught the words as she came in with a large platter of eggs and bacon and frowned. She must warn Rose not to pester her father. If he didn't feel the same towards Pearl as he did to Rose, it was a pity, and it was odd, too, but he couldn't help his feelings, she supposed, though it was a shame when you considered what a nice, quiet girl Pearl had become.

'It's all ready. Just call your sister again, will you, dear?' she said, and when Rose had gone out into the hall remarked cheerfully that Rose must be starving, as she had been out for an early swim and had looked quite blue afterwards.

At this information Miles frowned: 'It's too early in the year,' he said. 'Remember the attack of cramp she had.'

'I'm not likely to forget it – the scare it gave me; but don't say anything,' Kate advised. 'I've already reminded her. Rose is proud of being such a strong swimmer, and she would hate to give it up.'

Miles said irritably that he was making no such suggestion, but that Rose could well wait until it was warmer. With relief he realized that breakfast at last being ready there would be an end to this awkward questioning.

'Is Pearl coming?' Kate asked, as Rose returned.

'Yes. She answered me.' Rose was now in an obstinate mood which although comparatively rare, her mother recognized.

'Mummy, I wish you'd make Daddy realize that we like having her here.'

'But he knows we do,' Kate soothed. 'Pearl is a sweet girl; so helpful and friendly. She may have had a temper as a child, which was no more than might have been expected

28

with her Spanish blood, but she's quite got over it.'

'All children work themselves up into tantrums,' said Rose. 'I did myself, and you'd scarcely believe the carry-on there is with some of them at the school. They hate to be crossed.'

Children learnt self-control as they grew up, Kate opined, and one had to make allowances. 'Your Dad,' she said, 'always did act as though there was something different about Pearl, but although what happened was unfortunate, I know I could have managed her, if I'd been given a second chance, for I . . .'

She broke off as Pearl came in. How soft-footed the girl was, even though she wore high enough heels, higher even than those Rose bought. But though it was quite likely, thought Kate, that Pearl had overheard her remark or part of it she smiled at her unembarrassed, for she would just as readily have said them to her face.

'Ah, there you are, dear, you must be hungry for your breakfast, up so early as you were.'

'Well – for tea and toast anyway,' Pearl agreed, eyeing the big dish of bacon and eggs with disfavour.

The other three demolished what seemed to her to be an enormous meal each morning, and they in turn spoke of her lack of enthusiasm for breakfast as a Continental fashion.

Pearl sat down beside Rose, and Kate, about to pour milk into her cup before adding the tea, suddenly checked herself. Pearl smiled at her.

'One day you'll remember,' she said.

'After three months it's about time I did,' Kate admitted, 'but it seems so queer to take tea without milk or sugar. Still, we don't have to worry as long as that's the only way in which you're different.'

'Different?' Pearl enquired, taking her tea cup.

Kate explained : 'I was just saying when you came in that your Dad always behaved as though you were. When you were a little thing, I mean.'

Pearl looked at Miles – a cool, appraising glance. 'Oh, did he?' she said slowly.

'I couldn't see it myself; not during the short while you lived with us. I had to humour you a bit, but then you have to with all children. Anyway, you've grown up to be a nice, quiet girl with pretty manners, just the same as Rose and most

29

of her girl-friends.'

Pearl stretched out her hand to the toast rack, took a piece of toast and buttered it. An ironical smile flickered around her lips. She looked across the table at Miles, and it was as though her steady gaze compelled his. 'Yes – of course I have, just the same,' she said.

Had Miles not stifled his sigh, it would probably have sounded more akin to a groan. This couldn't go on. The tension was too great. He must have things out with Pearl; come to an understanding with her.

CHAPTER 5

The opportunity came that morning, for Kate and Rose went off together to do the weekend shopping, and Pearl stayed behind to tidy up. Miles settled down with the newspapers by the sunny window, but he was aware of Pearl's presence about the place; occasionally heard her light footfall. The day had warmed up by the time she came in with his mid-morning cup of coffee which she set down on a small table beside him.

'Kate and Rose have a good morning for their shopping,' she observed. 'They always enjoy dropping in at Fergus's for coffee, and meeting Brightwell people for a gossip.'

'You don't care for that sort of thing?'

'Oh yes, now and again. I sometimes do the weekend shopping, but Kate and Rose get more fun out of it. I shall probably take out a boat this afternoon. I like that better than anything. One feels so alone – only the sea and the sky.'

'It's solitary at this time of year, but there will be plenty of boats out later when the tourist season starts,' Miles remarked.

He drank his coffee which was good, and surveyed Pearl thoughtfully. She was undoubtedly a beautiful girl, and it was an unusual beauty. Now that she had recovered from her grief over Cynthia's death she was probably better looking than she had been when she was very young. There was a bloom upon her; she looked rested and tranquil. Her body in itself was a lovely thing; her smooth, golden skin, and her long eyes of a clear, hazel shade were set deep above high cheek-bones. The skin, the full mouth, the short, rather broad nose were legacies from her mother, but the light eyes and hair were reproductions of his own. From him, also, she inherited her height. He had been good-looking when he was her age, Miles reflected with passing complacency; more Nordic in appearance than most Englishmen; and he hadn't worn too badly, he supposed, for he was still thin and lithe, and his hair only lightly touched with grey.

'I shan't like Brightwell so much then,' said Pearl.

She stood up against the lintel of the window, looking down at him. Her attitude was reposeful, she never fidgeted, was rarely outwardly restless, though Miles was convinced that restlessness surged beneath the calm façade.

'No, you won't,' he said. 'We get crowded then, and they're not the sort of folk who will interest you; stolid Northerners, bent on having a good time while the weather lasts.'

'Well?' the monosyllable though quietly uttered, challenged.

'I'm warning you as you've not been here during the summer.'

'You think I can't mix with ordinary people?'

'I think you'll be bored.'

'Kate isn't – neither is Rose. They love Brightwell. Kate says it's heaven after living in Northpond, though you were sure she would miss town life.'

As though, thought Miles, there was any comparison between Kate's tastes and Pearl's. He said : 'Kate has made friends with the neighbours and has settled down. Rose has her interests too. She was lucky getting her position at the school here, with David only half a mile away. It's different for you. You can live anywhere you choose. Cynthia did the right thing in leaving you well provided for. You can rent a flat in London or stay in Paris or the South of France.'

'So I can,' said Pearl amicably.

'If you're bored you should consider some profession. You're clever, Pearl. You could study for a degree.'

She shook her head : 'I'm a bit old for that – nearly twenty-six.'

'Well, there's art. Cynthia said you painted and had talent.'

'Not really – Christmas card stuff.'

'If you took it up seriously, you might improve.'

Pearl sighed. She said gently : 'Why are you so anxious to get rid of me?'

'That's an unfair thing to say.'

'But you are – aren't you?'

'I'm only pointing out that there's nothing here for you.'

Pearl said : 'I have a home, a father, a sister and a kind step-mother. Kate and Rose have made me very welcome.'

'I know they have,' Miles unwillingly agreed.

Pearl looked at him reflectively. Miles had the sense of being summed up by one who realized his weakness, but who would be only too glad to make allowances for it. 'Why did you ask me here when Aunt Cynthia died?' enquired Pearl.

'You were very much alone and worn out with nursing her, but now after three months . . .'

'You have had enough of me.'

'I've not said so.'

Miles got up, went to his desk, found his tobacco-pouch and stood there filling his pipe. 'You're afraid to say anything definite, Father.'

But that wasn't true, Miles thought. It had been precisely because he intended to say something definite that he had allowed this conversation to take place, had encouraged it. But how could he explain to Pearl? It was impossible, for he had nothing but a faulty instinct to guide him; the instinct which warned him that she was dangerous, a trouble maker, though possibly an innocent and unconscious one. It was strange to be so deeply distrustful of a being he loved, of whom he was proud, though with a curious, thwarted pride. She was the type of woman fated to be a man's eternal torment, and he had brought her into the world.

After a moment he said sullenly : 'It was Kate who wanted you to come here. Personally I never expected it to work.'

'But it has. She's a nice woman, and we get on very well together.'

'You seem to.'

'You kept me apart from her for years – and from Rose,'

Pearl accused. 'It wasn't only because of the knife throwing, though that gave you an excuse. Until I was nearly twelve, I was safely accounted for, at a boarding school where I was happy enough – where you intended me to stay, except for holidays with Aunt Cynthia, until I was grown-up. But then Miss Fisher was ill and retired and closed down, and as Aunt Cynthia was going on tour to South Africa you were puzzled what to do with me. You said that I could live with you all at Northpond. Was that also due to Kate?'

It had indeed been Kate's doing, Miles remembered. Not that he had been unwilling to have his child with him, but he might have been afraid, might have resisted and found another school for her, only that Kate seemed so shocked. Pearl was his own child, she had reasoned, it was his duty to treat her as he treated Rose, to give her a proper home. Against his better judgement he had given way.

'Kate has a big heart,' he said.

'Yes, she's the type who should have had several children.'

'It wasn't our fault that we didn't.'

True enough that, he reflected. It had been the sorrow of Kate's life. She had wanted a large family of boys and girls, but though she appeared to be strong and healthy, she had brought Rose into the world with difficulty, and after that there had been an operation, which was essential, but had meant there would be no further babies. Perhaps it was chiefly because of this Kate had so often regretted that Pearl lived with his sister Cynthia.

'Pearl, I know it must be hard for you to understand me,' he said. 'You think I don't care for you . . .'

Pearl laughed; low but confident. 'I understand you very well, Father. I know you care for me.'

'You do, eh?'

'Though you wouldn't let me live with you when I was small, you couldn't keep away from me. At school you often came to see me. We had lovely times. Don't you remember the zoo and the pantomime and taking me out to tea; stuffing me with cream buns. I couldn't understand then why we weren't always together.'

'Cynthia wanted you in the holidays, and you were happy with her.'

'Happier with you, Father.'

There was a poignancy in this, in her low voice, which wrenched his heart; stirred him to remorse. 'Oh, my dear,' he said helplessly.

'I used to think how wonderful it would be if we could be always together, and when Miss Fisher closed the school and you took me because Aunt Cynthia would be far away, I was in heaven. But nothing came about as I expected, for Kate and Rose were more important to you. Naturally, I was jealous, and then Rose and I fought. Aunt Cynthia was home again by then, and she was able to take me. I had nine months with you as a child, and now I've had another three.'

'I know you reproach me,' said Miles.

'Reproach! Not exactly. I've always been a problem to you. Even though I was responsible for the scar on Rose's cheek, you must have been glad, for it settled matters. You then had good reason for sending me away.'

'It was the only thing to do.'

'But after that happened, Rose and I could have been friends. I was so bitterly sorry and ashamed.'

Miles realized he had no right, no reason to doubt her sincerity, but his recollection of that long-ago scene was vivid, and different from hers. She recalled a penitent child, who had caused an injury in an outburst of temper, which Rose's temper had matched; but he remembered that while Rose had sobbed with anger and wailed with pain, Pearl had been silent, watching her wounded sister with an unchildlike pleasure in her eyes. If there had been sorrow and shame it had not been there when blood trickled down Rose's cheek and Kate had screamed in panic.

'According to my lights I did my best for you,' he said. 'It was difficult in some ways when I married again. Kate was young and for a time very delicate. Rose was as much as she could manage and Cynthia was only too anxious to have you.'

'And you only too anxious to put the past behind you.'

'Very well then, I admit it. Rightly or wrongly, I was.'

Pearl turned away from him. She said: 'Aunt Cynthia often talked to me about my mother. She wasn't ashamed of her.'

'Neither was I!'

The words flashed back with the accent of truth. Ashamed? No; what he felt was quite different. His first marriage had been a bitter mistake, as much a mistake for the beautiful doomed child he had made his wife, as it was for him. Love had sprung up between them with a consuming flame. He could have saved her from it had he been less headstrong, had he left her while there was yet time to leave her. It would have been bitter pain, but less than that which marriage had brought upon them.

'That's hard to believe,' said Pearl scornfully, 'considering the nonsense you must have told Kate. I've listened to her a dozen times, and I've wanted to tell her the truth. But I'm such a fool I couldn't nerve myself to give you away. A Spanish lady!'

Miles winced. Though Pearl believed she loved him, it was a love, he thought, which emotionally was nearer to hate. And what was his love for her? If she went out of his life tomorrow, if he never saw her again, would his relief be greater than regret, a sense of loss? He did not know.

'Young people do crazy things,' he said. 'When I married your mother I was some years younger than you are now.'

'And she was only a child.'

'Not by their standards; girls of her race mature early, and in some ways she had wisdom. But she did not look ahead — neither did I. All we thought was that life would be impossible without each other. I can't explain it to you, Pearl ... it wasn't as though she was an ignorant girl, besides being extraordinarily beautiful, she had also been well educated. She had had an English governess and spoke the language perfectly.'

Pearl sat down in the chair opposite to him. Her face was alight with interest, her eyes fixed eagerly upon him. She said : 'Aunt Cynthia told me she was connected with a royal house who were wiped out in a local uprising.'

'That's quite true. Her governess saved her when the rest of her family were slaughtered. She was taken to an English mission and they kept her there; had her baptized and confirmed. We were married in the mission church.'

Pearl watched him as he paced the room, realizing that he was re-living that scene of so many years ago; but she did not realize how often Miles recalled it. The exquisite face of

35

his bride, misty through the net veil; her small body in the white sheath of a gown, and round her neck and on her arms the jewel-studded chains which were her dowry.

These, the devoted governess who had saved her had caught up and concealed when she had smuggled the child out of the palace and had brought her to safety. Miles supposed that Pearl now possessed these; they had been given into Cynthia's care, and he knew she had handed them over to Pearl when she was twenty-one. But he had never seen her wear them.

At the mission they had been proud of the child they had reared. The pastor and his wife had loved her devotedly. If he had gone off without her, they would have helped her to bear her misery; but he hadn't been able to forgo her. She had seemed so much more desirable than any English girl. He had been enthralled by her beauty, the exquisite fragility of her, the look of race and pride.

'Did nobody try to dissuade you?' Pearl asked.

'I wouldn't listen to them. I was crazy about her. The — well the uncivilized element didn't strike me at the time. I was fool enough to think I could mould her, make her what I wanted her to be, and I only found out my mistake when it was too late.'

Mould her! Later, he had groaned at his crass folly, his certainty that she was no different from any other young and inexperienced girl. It had not struck him then that her race, her dynasty, irrevocably separated them in spirit, though physically they were so well mated.

'What did she do?' asked Pearl.

'Do?'

'Obviously your efforts to make her over again were unsuccessful.'

Reluctantly, yet determined to make her understand something of what he had endured, Miles said : 'From the first it was impossible. When we were coming home on the ship everyone admired her. There was a dance on board, and some fellow tried to make love to her. She nearly killed him; stuck a dagger into him. Luckily it was only a flesh wound, but there was the hell of a to-do about it.'

Pearl laughed — sharply, without amusement. 'Naturally there would be, but in time she might have learnt that such excessive virtue was redundant.'

36

'It wasn't only that. She wanted the chap to die. She couldn't forgive him or forget about it. She said he had defiled her, and when he fell ill she tried to put a spell on him, so that he wouldn't recover.'

'Did she succeed?'

'No. I discovered in time what she was at. She made a wax image. Of course it was all nonsense, but the chap wasn't getting better. He had a fever, some sort of infection . . .'

Miles broke off, regretting now that he had told her of this incident, but Pearl was vividly interested. She said: 'Go on,' in a tense voice, and Miles tried to explain chaotic emotions which defied explanation.

'I couldn't really blame her,' he said. 'I knew we were up against something that was inherent in her which she probably understood no more than I did. Besides, in a way, I had to admire her loyalty. But it shows how little Christian teaching counted. Underneath, she was as primitive as any other native girl.'

'What did you do?' asked Pearl.

'Reasoned with her, pleaded with her, at last told her that if she didn't lay off, I should send her away and never see her again. I convinced her that I meant it. She couldn't understand but she obeyed me.'

In the past, Pearl had listened attentively to all that her aunt could tell her about her unknown mother, but this was a new light thrown upon her character. All Pearl's sympathies were with the desolate little bride, but that did not prevent her from seeing things from Miles's standpoint. Impossible to imagine how this strange marriage would have resolved itself had her mother lived.

'I was never sure of her afterwards, though I passed it over,' said Miles.

'But I dare say she noticed a difference – a kind of repugnance,' Pearl suggested.

Miles sighed: 'Perhaps she did – poor child. I was thankful to get her off that boat. People were avoiding her by then, whispering they were sorry for me. Well, you couldn't wonder at it. One woman, a nice soul too, asked me if the marriage was really legal; if I couldn't do something about it. When we were home and Cynthia accepted her, raved about

37

her in fact, it was an enormous relief.'

'It must have been. Dear Aunt Cynthia, she was always a romantic.'

And as unlike Miles as was possible. It was difficult to believe they were so closely related. Cynthia was generous and kind and tolerant. She had loved the little dark bride and had been good to her. She had seen the beauty of her character; the mystery which went with it only made her more interesting. Pearl knew that Cynthia had despised Miles because by then he was frightened, because he was thinking that he had made a disastrous mistake.

Pearl looked at her father and wondered. He had been a young man then, and must have had a tendency to adventure. How was it that he had not been proud of his beautiful wife, whose devotion he had so entirely won, and delighted because she was different from the placid young women of his home town?

As for her mother, thought Pearl, her infatuation was easy to understand, for when Miles was young he must have looked splendid, with his fair hair and athletic body. To the little Indian Princess he must have seemed god-like.

Miles went on in his stilted, embarrassed manner: 'We knew by then that you were on the way and your mother was happy about it. Cynthia was older than I by nine years, and she had already made her mark on the stage. Our parents were dead, but I had the factory. I had been threatened with lung illness, that was what took me to foreign parts, but I had to get going when I returned. I spent my time between Northpond and Cynthia's flat, leaving your mother there.'

Pearl remembered all that her aunt had told her of those waiting months. The child, as she had called Pearl's mother, had been so patient and so silent. She had spent long hours working on her baby's layette, doing the fine needlework she had been taught to do at the mission station; reading, taking long, shivering walks in the park, because this had been recommended by the doctor. But on the days when Miles was expected she had bloomed, had sung softly round the house, had worn her prettiest dresses and her jewels. All she had needed or had asked was to be near him.

'Aunt Cynthia said that winter was very trying to her,' Pearl said. 'She told me she caught cold upon cold; that the climate was unbearable for her. She said that when she was dying she knew it, but she was not afraid.'

'She came of a stoical race.'

'Aunt Cynthia said I was a plain likeness of her, except for my fair hair. That's one reason why you hate having me around. I remind you of her.'

Sitting down heavily in an armchair, Miles denied this. 'I don't hate having you around.'

'How different it must have been when you married Kate.' Pearl's voice was amused. 'I've seen photographs. A nice, plump, placid girl with a curly fringe. My mother had long, black hair which fell to her knees. It was as fine as silk. She had tiny hands and feet and a mouth like a rose. Aunt Cynthia said the most graceful of actresses never moved on the stage as she moved – it reminded her of flowing water . . . and she worshipped you. She saw only you, heard only your voice; everything she had belonged to you; her beauty, her heart and her soul.'

'Don't,' Miles cried.

It was a torturingly true picture, and as Pearl portrayed it, he knew that momentarily at least, she hated him. Bewildered remorse nagged at him, not for what he had done to Pearl's mother, but for what he had done to their child. He had failed her and was failing her now, but he hadn't the slightest notion of how to alter matters. The love which existed between them had neither trust nor kindness in it. Better for them both had they coldly disliked each other, for Pearl knew that although he would suffer if he lost her, the suffering would be something he could accept, even welcome, and because of this, she would hurt him if she could.

'She was proud,' said Pearl, 'but for you she was humble. She had great nobility, but she had no fear of evil. She would have fed powdered glass to anyone who injured you and would have smiled to see them die in agony.'

Miles shuddered. He said : 'I believe she would.'

'Disconcerting certainly for a stolid Northern Englishman.'

Pearl was leaning now on the back of his chair. One hand

39

slipped down and touched his shoulder: 'Why are you saying these things?' Miles asked.

'To show you how well I understand her, to show you that in some ways I *am* her.'

But that touch of fantasy was too much for Miles. His mind seemed to clear suddenly, and he saw himself as a middle-aged fool, making far too much of the fact that he had married a girl of a different race. Pearl was no avenging goddess, but a young woman given to histrionics.

'Nonsense,' he said. 'You have had the advantage of an English upbringing and you are as much my daughter as you are hers.'

'You say it, but you don't believe it. Wouldn't you be sorry for any man who wanted to marry me? Wouldn't you feel it was your duty to prevent him?'

'Not if he knew the truth and accepted it, and you are sufficiently attractive to make any man who loved you accept far worse. Already there must have been men who have asked you to marry them?'

A few, Pearl admitted, but none of them had meant anything to her, and she reminded Miles that throughout the last few years she had had little time to think of herself. Looking after her aunt had occupied all her time.

'I shouldn't make a good wife,' she said. 'I'm too complex. I wish I wasn't. It would be peaceful to be like Rose. She has her plans all set, and the factory means almost as much to her as David. She'll be a credit to you, Father.'

Because there was wistfulness in her voice, Miles put up his hand and took hers which still rested on his shoulder.

'And so will you, my dear, be a credit to all who love you.'

'What, with my mixed blood which scares you? When I threw that knife at Rose would you have taken it so seriously had I been Kate's daughter?'

'Certainly I should. Impossible to have that sort of thing happening between two youngsters.'

Pearl laughed. She withdrew her hand from his, and came round from the back of the chair. She said: 'What a liar you are! But I love you for it.'

'It's no lie. Just now it came upon me that we've been making too much of the whole thing.'

'I wonder.' Pearl went to the window, gazed out of it, and then drew back from it : 'That's David – he's just driven up in that new horseless carriage he's bought.'

Miles rose to join her at the window with a relief which he could not disguise.

✳ CHAPTER 6 ✳

David Page had read in novels of the hero or heroine awaking one morning to find themselves famous, and occasionally he had wondered how one would react to such an experience. Now, in a small way, he thought he knew.

His mother had been dead for many years and his father was not particularly interested in what he referred to as 'David's literary activities'. But the elderly housekeeper who had looked after them for years was thrilled and excited.

She had brought David a sheaf of papers while he was still in bed, and she had gloated over him while he read them. She adored him, for he had been only a boy in his teens when he had been left to her care, and in her opinion he was far too good for the factory which mattered more to his father than did David himself.

Neither Kate nor Rose greatly appealed to her. Mrs Reever was a Londoner, and people who lived elsewhere were classed in her mind as 'provincials'. Mr David, she thought, could have done better than tie himself up to such an ordinary girl.

Had David's father realized that she fostered his son's ambitious dreams, he would have been gravely disturbed, but he had no idea of it. To him the quiet, ageing woman was nondescript, and he little knew that David had read his play and other earlier unsuccessful ones to her, scene by scene, and had been admiringly praised for them. Not that David took that too seriously, though he admitted it was welcome. It had been due to Mrs Reever that he had entered his play for the Arts prize, and when he won it, he had been touched and oddly humbled by her delight.

41

Now because the notices were so good, she was jubilant. She had been at the theatre the night before and had been so proud of him she had wanted to tell everyone she had read the play long before it had been submitted for the competition.

Too loyal to her employer to say so, she secretly hoped it would be the beginning of a new life for David. Surely his father would now have to see that he was worthy of something more suitable than a business career at the factory which plainly bored him. There would have been more hope for him, as she realized, had Rose Shandon been a different type of girl, but with or without Rose she was convinced that David was more than ordinarily gifted and would make a name for himself.

This morning David listened to her and laughed, but he half believed her. He was far from expecting immediate fame, but one day he might be known and might be able to give up his position at the factory, the blow softened for his father because he was doing well in a different sphere. He realized, as did Mrs Reever, that much depended on Rose to whom he was sincerely attached. It was difficult to assess her reactions. Last night she had been excited and pleased. She could not well be otherwise, surrounded by so many people who were praising him and wishing him well. The party afterwards at a hotel in Northpond had been highly successful, and they had all enjoyed themselves. But when he thought back to that party, it was the face of Rose's half-sister, Pearl, which stood out most clearly.

Pearl was a lovely girl and naturally he had, during the last three months, shared the general interest in her. Hers was the kind of beauty an artist might want to paint. This David instinctively recognized.

Rose had confided to him her belief that her father was not too well pleased to have Pearl staying with them. There was some mystery about Pearl or so Rose suspected. It couldn't be solely because of the childish quarrel in which she had been injured that Miles sometimes seemed cold and hostile to his older daughter.

Pearl must have been a passionate child, David reflected, though she was now so cool and self-controlled; but when he watched her vivid changes of expression and the light in

42

her eyes he was sure they reflected a temperament which few fathomed. Last night he had seen her roused to enthusiasm. The play had meant something to her; this he had known when she had taken his hand to congratulate him. She had said it was the kind of play one would not easily forget, and she had questioned him, had asked him if it was his first attempt, and how he had come to write it.

Rose had been surrounded by friends and he and Pearl had been isolated for a short while, and they talked. He had been keenly aware of her bright, intelligent eyes, her glowing beauty. She made everyone else seem colourless.

It was odd that Miles Shandon had married the type of woman to produce Pearl, for to David he seemed commonplace; an agreeable man and certainly a good-looking one, but it was difficult to think of him marrying a Spanish girl. He had heard it said that she had been highly bred, and he had known that such girls were closely guarded, almost cloistered. David wondered if it had been a runaway match, an elopement, but such flamboyance was very unlike the man now known to him, the man for whom Kate seemed an excellent and fitting partner. It struck him for the first time that Pearl's features, her short, blunt nose, soft full mouth and high cheek-bones, were not usually associated with Spanish beauty.

It was of no particular importance. Whatever her ancestry on her mother's side, Pearl herself was a wonderful person. He remembered how Rose had told him of her devoted attendance on her paralysed aunt. Few girls would have been willing to give up over two years to nursing an invalid who had become more helpless with every week that passed.

David wondered about her now, as he had wondered about her before. She was so beautiful that it was odd she should be unattached at nearly twenty-six. Several of his Northpond friends had asked to be introduced to her, but they had appeared to make no headway with her. They found her elusive; polite but not interested.

His thoughts veered as he came within sight of the Shandons' bungalow, and shortly afterwards he pulled up his motor car outside the gate. He was immensely proud of it, and because he drove it with skill and some speed was regarded by his friends as a pioneer. Rose was only doubtfully approving.

43

She had much preferred the horse and dog-cart which had preceded the motor. However, they were good companions as well as engaged lovers, and David always enjoyed his week-ends. They passed too swiftly, and he rarely failed to wake on a Monday morning without a sense of despondency, for then the week with its long hours at the factory, for which try as he did he could feel no enthusiasm, stretched before him.

It was his engagement to Rose which made such a life tolerable. He looked forward to sharing a home with her, and that incentive urged him on to satisfy both their fathers.

The old-fashioned house in which he lived was dark and heavily furnished. His father would allow no alterations, and he and David had never been companionable, for Joseph Page had the tastes of a recluse; but at Rose's home it was different. There were generally plenty of young people about. Rose liked to have visitors, liked to dance and to play tennis. She enjoyed gardening, enjoyed making plans for their future home. It was unfortunate that she cared so little for reading, and laughed at him because he could not have too many books as possessions; but he supposed few girls were any different.

Pearl was though. He had realized that last night. He went up the garden path with the thought in his mind that he would see Pearl again today and perhaps have the chance to talk to her.

Miles Shandon opened the long window for him to enter, and David glancing round the room met the gaze of the girl who had occupied his recent thoughts. Miles told him that Rose had gone shopping with her mother, and that she had left a message for David to wait for her.

David listened and agreed. Nobody would have supposed that he only vaguely heard Miles. He was looking at Pearl in her dark, plain dress, and could almost have believed that he saw her for the first time. He asked : 'How are you feeling after a late night?'

She smiled : 'Splendid. Have you seen the notices of the play?'

'Yes. They amazed me. I didn't expect anything half so good.'

'But the play had a fine reception.'

'Oh well! I doubt if that counted for much. There were so many in the audience who are our personal friends; they wouldn't be likely to throw rotten eggs at me.'

'But you were the prize-winner and there were lots of entries.'

'Very few of them were even passable, so I'm told. Nine people out of ten think they can write plays. As Rose says, it's a nice hobby,' and David laughed good humouredly.

'That's because – for you – she doesn't want it to be anything more.'

It was as though Pearl was trying to tell him something, David thought, which could not be said because Miles was present. With a smile as he recalled Rose's insistence that work and play – and for her writing was no more than play – should be kept apart, David said : 'I know.'

'Rose has your best interests at heart,' Miles reminded him. 'It wouldn't do for you to get too wrapped up in play-writing. There's no future in it.'

'On an average she has told me that six times a day for the last six weeks.' David's smile was now tinged with ruefulness, and Pearl made a slight gesture which could have been interpreted either as annoyance or regret.

'There's no harm in it so long as it's only a sideline,' Miles allowed.

'Under the circumstances it can't be anything else,' David observed.

'Why not?' asked Pearl.

'If I wanted to be a successful playwright, I should have to give my whole life to it, and even then I might not succeed.'

'You probably wouldn't,' said Miles.

Pearl remonstrated : 'How defeatist you are. At the beginning few writers can give all their time to their work, but they can as they get on. I thought it a remarkable play – a play to make one think and hope. Surely, David, you won't let it rest here; you will try it elsewhere?'

'I might send it around,' David said doubtfully. 'But I'm told managers are rarely encouraging. I wrote another play about a year ago, and couldn't get anyone to look at it.'

Mrs Reever had been his sole audience when he read it aloud. A very satisfactory one, for she had been certain he was a genius.

Pearl said : 'I could give you an introduction to a manager who is a friend of mine.'

'A London manager?'

'Graham Bernard,' said Pearl.

The name meant nothing to Miles, but it meant a great deal to David. His face lit up in vivid interest, became alert and alive. And that, thought Pearl, was how he should look. It was an interesting face, if not a handsome one; a face that was too thin, with dark eyes which were sombre; a flexible, sensitive mouth; a bony nose.

'Bernard's the manager of the Corinthian,' said David.

'I know him quite well,' Pearl said lightly. 'Graham was fond of Aunt Cynthia and visited her every week until the end.'

It awed David to hear anyone speak of the great man in such an airy, casual way. He knew that Cynthia Shandon had once been a celebrated actress, but the family referred to her in such a deprecating manner that he had scarcely taken it in; much less had he paused to consider that Pearl had probably met people from all grades of the theatre world.

'If you would put me in touch with him, it would be wonderful,' he said.

Miles looking from one to the other, broke in discouragingly. 'Well, I don't pretend to be a judge,' he said, 'and I don't want to be damping, but in my opinion it would be wise to call it a day. I was naturally interested in your play when I saw it last night, but it's not up to professional standard.'

'There could be two opinions about that,' said Pearl gently.

Miles became pompous, and not the less so because he realized that this must be how he appeared to David and Pearl. He said : 'From time to time I've seen most of the London successes, when I had to be up there on business. Your play, David, could not stand up to them, and for another thing it's not your job. I'd be the last to grudge you relaxation, but I'd be better pleased to see you take up golf or tennis. You are only laying up disappointment for yourself, if you get too absorbed in writing.'

David said : 'I can take disappointment.'

Pearl believed that was true. Until now, David's whole life must have been disappointing. Except for his brief years at college, except for the friends he had made, he had endured unnatural repression. Even Rose, when she spoke of Joseph Page, was indignant. When David's mother had died, her husband had sunk into melancholy and his one outlet was the factory. David had been well educated, well clothed, well fed, but nobody had cared much about him except the housekeeper.

'There's the danger you won't leave your love of play-writing behind you during work hours,' Miles went on. 'Your father and I are pleased with the progress you have made this last year, the way in which you have dug in your heels, but you've a long way yet to go, and there are wasted years you have to make up.'

There was no opportunity for David to answer, to vindicate himself if he could, for the front door was heard to open and in came Kate and Rose, rather tired, slightly breathless, and laden with shopping baskets. When she saw David, Rose put her shopping basket on the floor and ran to him and kissed him.

'Oh darling, have you been waiting long?' she said. 'It's turned into a really warm day. I'm sorry I was out. We expected to be back before now, but so many people stopped us to talk about the play. Half Brightwell must have been at the theatre last night.'

Kate unbuttoned her coat and sank into an easy chair. 'Goodness, I'm hot,' she said. 'We just couldn't get along, for we were held up again and again. Everyone liked your speech, David. They thought you were so natural.'

David said, amused : 'I was in a perfectly natural funk.'

Rose gave him another hug and then stood beside him with her hand in his. 'Oh well, it's all over now,' she said, 'and I must say I'm thankful. We have had enough of the limelight. Now we can get on with ordinary things and be happy again.'

'But Rose, dear,' Kate said, 'surely David's little success hasn't made you unhappy?'

'It unsettled me,' said Rose.

David looked down at her fondly, but also with an unusual determination. He said: 'I can't quite write it off like that. There's a chance that it may be seen in London.'

Instantly Rose was on the alert. 'Who says so?'

'Pearl is friendly with Graham Bernard, the manager of the Corinthian Theatre, and she says she will give me a letter of introduction to him. It's unlikely he'll think anything of the play, but it's worth a try.'

There was a short silence which David recognized as hostile. Then Rose said slowly, her gaze resting on her sister: 'I wish you hadn't brought Pearl into this.'

'I brought myself into it,' Pearl retorted lightly. 'I offered to do anything I could. Graham will pay attention to my opinion – he's done so before now. When the script of *Youth's Manuscript* was sent to him, I read it and advised him to produce it.'

'But that ran in London for over a year,' said David.

'It ran for fifteen months.'

'Oh David,' cried Rose in distress, 'must you send it? Suppose this man has it put on?'

'You goose!' David pressed her hand close to his side. 'That's what I'm hoping he will do, though there's scarcely a chance.'

In a serene voice Pearl contradicted him. 'There's a very good chance.'

Rose uttered a slight, whimpering sound and David said tenderly: 'You silly little thing. I might make a lot of money. I might be able to buy you a real pearl necklet.'

'But I don't want one. I want you to be a partner and director of the factory.'

'What's to prevent me, even if the play does get a London production?'

It was a reasonable question, but Miles said on a note of harshness: 'Lack of interest in your work here will prevent you.'

'It will, David – it will really,' Rose cried.

'You have improved,' Miles allowed, 'but you haven't yet mastered your job.'

'I've done my best.'

Now there was a note of sullenness in David's voice and

Pearl's sympathy for him was shot with regret. That note wasn't the right one; he should be calm and confident and determined. But how could one expect as much, when hers was the first real encouragement he had ever received?

'I'm not disputing it,' said Miles. 'It made a great difference when Rose took you in hand; but you can't afford to be half-hearted; not if you are to be made junior partner when you marry Rose next year.'

'It's so terribly important to us, darling,' Rose pleaded.

'I know,' David reluctantly agreed.

'Concentration is what you most need,' said Miles.

David threw him a resentful glance. Did this family and his own father think he belonged to them body and soul?

'Go in for something that takes you out of doors; something healthy. I'll be straight with you, David. Unless I know where I am with you, I shall persuade your father to defer your partnership and I shall advise Rose to postpone marrying you.'

'Oh, Daddy!' Rose's voice was a wail.

David looked down upon her face puckered with anxiety and distress and his heart softened to her. The poor little thing; this wasn't fair on her. It would have given him nothing but pleasure to have defied Miles, to tell him he could defer the confounded partnership until the end of time, so far as he was concerned, but he couldn't say such a thing before Rose. She had been so sweet to him. Even before they were actually in love she had been sweet to him. He had been lonely and at odds with the world, and Rose had gone out of her way to be kind, to take his part, to make him welcome at her home. He had poured out his grievances to her and she had listened and sympathized; she had shown so much interest in him, that he had started to make the best of things, to pull his weight at the factory in order to please her. A few months ago it had all seemed satisfying. Rose had been sufficiently interested in his writing, and at that time David had merely thought it would be fun to write a play now and again for amateurs. But now it was different. He had put his best into the play which had won the prize; he had taken enormous pleasure in it, and real ambition had stirred in him, an ambition which Pearl had fanned.

'It's for your own good, Rose,' Miles was saying. 'I have to

49

consider your future.'

'Isn't that rather drastic?' David asked coldly.

'Maybe, but sometimes one has the need of a firm hand. Up to now I've been pretty lenient. I wasn't too keen on Rose tying herself up, but I agreed because I liked you, and I hoped it would help you to pull yourself together.'

'But he has, Daddy – you know he has,' Rose cried.

'He has made a good start. Don't let him spoil it now.'

'Oh David, you won't, will you?' Rose anxiously implored him.

Even as he looked down at her with tenderness, with compassion and understanding, David was conscious of the silent Pearl. He could not have put a name to her expression, but he knew she was willing him to resist.

'You want me to give up writing altogether?' he asked.

'No,' said Miles, 'not altogether. I'm a reasonable man I hope, but you can put it aside for the time being. You need to put your serious work first. It's your livelihood and Rose's too. What you have to think about is making a home for yourselves. Rose has her heart set on being married next year and living near us and all her friends.'

'I'd hate to have our wedding postponed,' Rose said in a broken voice. 'I've told everyone and I don't want to go on teaching. I want my own home. I want to make everything lovely for you. Oh David, I want us both to be safe.' Sobs choked her as she uttered the last words, and tears started to pour down her cheeks. It was with passion that she cried: 'Don't throw it all away – please don't. If you do, I think my heart will break.'

Never had David seen her in such a state; his calm, capable managing Rose. He hated both Miles and himself for so throwing her off balance. As she soobbed and clung to him, the violence of her distress frightened him.

'Rose – oh, come, Rose, this isn't like you,' he soothed.

'I can't be everlastingly sensible and controlled and placid,' Rose wept. 'Sometimes everything gets too much for me. I don't know how to put it to you, how to make you understand. This means so much to us. I know Daddy has given you good advice – if only you could believe it, if only you could trust me to know what is best for us.'

She had the sense of throwing herself against an unyielding wall. She couldn't believe that this was David, her David who was resisting her. Everything had been going so beautifully, they had been so sure of each other, and now all was changed. David held her closely, not speaking. His glance roved to Pearl, but now her head was downbent, and he thought she seemed almost indifferent; but Rose was pleading with all her heart and soul, and he was incapable of denying her. With a deep sigh he surrendered : 'All right then, you win !' he said.

Relief flashed across her tear-wet face. 'You mean you do trust Daddy to know what is best.'

'I suppose so.'

Kate, who had not ventured to speak, but whose expression had mirrored her dismay, rose and approached them. 'Well now, that's very sensible of you, David,' she approved. 'Upon my word, such a scene ! Stop crying, Rose, there's a dear. Here's a clean handkerchief. You've about soaked yours.'

Blind with tears, Rose accepted the handkerchief, and dabbed at her streaming eyes, and Kate, thinking it was about time somebody said something practical and put an end to unnecessary emotion, went on to remark in a comfortably commonplace fashion that she would have to get the vegetables on, and that of course David would stay to dinner. He hesitated and looked at Rose : 'I've the motor here,' he said, 'and I had planned to take Rose out for a meal.'

'Not a bad idea,' Miles said heartily. 'You take her out and make a fuss of her.'

'What about it, Rose ?' asked David.

Rose, with her breath still coming in quivering gasps, was understood to say that she would like it, and David, having committed himself was only anxious to get away from Rose's parents. When she said something about being untidy, he turned up her face, took Kate's handkerchief and gently dried her eyes. 'Now you look grand,' he said. 'Come along.'

Obediently, exhausted by the tumultuous emotion so unlike her, Rose slipped her hand into his and went with him.

'Don't you be worrying your head about all this,' Kate said.

'I won't,' Rose promised.

David murmured a few polite words and assured Kate that he would not keep Rose out too late. Yes, he would be pleased to stay for supper, and would be back in good time for it. He did not look at Pearl. She must despise him. How could she do anything else?

'Well, that's that,' said Miles, as the motor was heard to drive off.

'You were most persuasive,' Pearl remarked drily.

'I want to do what's right by both of them.'

Pearl's expression might be hard to read, but Kate's was approving. 'Of course you do,' she said. 'I'm thankful you were here. That boy needs someone to talk sense to him.'

'Rose has set her heart on him,' said Miles, suppressing his conviction that David was not worthy of her.

Pearl picked up one of the papers, and once more read through the review of David's play. She said with little expression : 'Yes, she certainly has.'

❋ CHAPTER 7 ❋

Although David gave the impression of not being over strong, for he was too thin for his height, he rarely fell ill, and it was therefore a matter of concern to Mrs Reever when he went down with a severe attack of influenza only a few days after the production of his play. The doctor was told, and after seeing David said that he must stay in bed and would be off work for at least a week. David, although feeling hot and restless because his temperature had soared, was aware of relief.

In spite of his surrender there was strain between himself and Rose, but that, he thought, would probably have passed over by the time he was about again. Meanwhile it was a blessed reprieve to be unable to put in an appearance at the factory. He scribbled a note to Rose, forbidding her to visit him, pointing out that she might become infected if she came near him during the next week. She had her work at the school, and was at present hard at it coaching her form for their College of Preceptors examination, therefore she could not afford to be ill.

Rose was concerned, but agreed that it would be only sensible to keep away. She telephoned frequently and Mrs Reever reported on David's progress. She also wrote and sent flowers, magazines and fruit.

David, after the first two days of feeling sorry for himself, revelled in the peace. Mrs Reever thoroughly enjoyed herself, for now she could fuss over him as much as she wished. She cooked tempting, invalid food and told him every day that he should take his time about getting well; no good purpose would be served by going back to work before he was thoroughly fit. David was in entire agreement.

It had turned cold and wet, which made him the more willing to stay indoors. He had his books and a fire in his room and was content. Each day his father paid him a brief visit, and then David took care to seem limp and weary, not conscious of any particular duplicity. It would be ages, he knew, before he was granted another such respite.

He had been in bed for nearly a week when Mrs Reever came to him looking slightly put out. A young lady had called : it was Miss Rose's half-sister, whom she had seen for the first time on the night David's play was produced.

A beautiful young lady, Mrs Reever grudgingly admitted. She had said that she was not afraid of germs, and that if Mr David was well enough she would very much like to see him.

'Of course I'm well enough,' said David eagerly, sitting bolt upright in bed, 'though I'd better brush myself up a bit. Mercifully I shaved this morning. Get me my dressing-gown, Reevy, like a dear.'

The dressing-gown was a blue Paisley silk and very smart. Mrs Reever had to smile as she brought it to him, and watched him as he brushed his hair and looked round the room to see if it was reasonably tidy. 'Miss Rose won't be too pleased to think you have seen her sister before seeing her,' she commented.

'Miss Rose need not be told,' said David. 'I expect Miss Shandon called on impulse, because she was shopping and near here.'

Mrs Reever admitted that Pearl had said something of the

sort, and when she had straightened the room according to David's directions, and had pulled the most comfortable chair near to the fire, she went downstairs and told Pearl that the invalid would be pleased to see her.

'But you won't stay too long, will you, Miss?' she said. 'It's only today that his temperature is down to normal, and it wouldn't do to over-tire him.'

Pearl promised to be careful so earnestly that Mrs Reever smiled upon her. Although she had enjoyed having David to herself, it was possible, she thought, that he was beginning to be bored and to feel lonely. She might have put up more opposition had Rose called, but she was impressed by Pearl, who to her approval carried grapes in a wicker basket and had a sheaf of carnations on her arm.

'These are for the invalid,' she said, having been ushered into David's room, 'though my business today is really with the playwright.'

David stared at her mutely, unable to stop staring, and Pearl laughed : 'What's the matter? Have I got smut on my nose?'

'I'd forgotten how beautiful you were,' said David. 'It's wonderful of you to come to see me, especially as Mrs Reever says it's a miserably cold day. Sit by the fire, and tea will be coming along in a minute.'

'That will be nice,' said Pearl. She sat in the big chair as directed and stretched out her slender feet to the warmth of the fire. She said : 'You don't look particularly ill.'

'I'm on the mend, but dear old Reevy fusses, and she'll keep me here as long as she can.'

'Rose worries about you,' said Pearl.

'But I write to her nearly every day.'

'She would be angry if she knew I had called to see you; but she needn't know. I thought it all out. I knew your father would be at the factory, and Rose is at her school. Nobody will disturb us for an hour, and I hoped you would be well enough to talk business.'

'Of course I'm well enough.'

A bemused sense of enchantment was stealing over David. This room would never seem quite the same now Pearl had sat in the big chair. He would constantly see her sitting there at her ease beside the fire, smiling at him.

54

Mrs Reever came in with the tea-tray and fussed about, putting it down on the table beside the bed, and then carrying both tray and table across the room to Pearl's side. Pearl thanked her sweetly. 'What a lovely tea. The cake looks gorgeous,' she said.

'Reevy is a wonder at cake-making,' David praised.

'Would you stay and have tea with us, Mrs Reever?' Pearl asked.

The gratified Mrs Reever refused, but offered to pour out for both of them, and Pearl accepted. Mrs Reever said : 'If you're hungry, Miss, I could cut you some ham sandwiches as well. I know Mr David wouldn't want them, as he had his lunch later than usual.'

Pearl said that the scones and the cake were a feast. 'I mean to have some of both, and not give a thought to my waistline.'

Mrs Reever told her admiringly that she had no need to, hers was the sort of figure that always stayed slim. David and Pearl laughed at this remark when the door had closed on the housekeeper. 'I can't imagine how she knows, but I hope it's true,' Pearl said.

'You've enslaved her,' said David. 'She couldn't take her eyes off you. She's a dear soul and I think the world of her, but Rose thinks she is too possessive.'

'Why shouldn't she be? She's looked after you for years, hasn't she? From all I hear you would have been forlorn without her.'

Rose had made her easy capture, thought Pearl, because he had been so desolate. Her affectionate ways, and the bright and cheerful home to which she introduced him, must have made a great difference to his life.

David was too enchanted by his visitor to feel hungry, but Pearl ate with appetite, finding that the scones and cake tasted even better than they looked.

'I want to talk about the play,' she said, when Mrs Reever had taken away the tray. 'You have a copy of it here, I suppose?'

'There's one over there in the desk.'

'I saw it again at the Arts last night, David. I felt I must before it comes off on Saturday. The others thought I had gone to the cinema. To be truthful, I admit I was rather

55

nervous. A first night show can be misleading. People are excited and inclined to think a play is better than it really is. I, myself, was so astonished to find it good that I realized I might have over-rated it. I wanted to be sure. I knew I could be unbiased seeing it for a second time.'

'And how did you react?' David asked anxiously.

'I thought it even better than when I saw it on the opening night. There was an excellent house, and the players had all got into their stride. I was enthralled.'

'You don't know how much it means to me to hear you say that.'

'Well, now the thing is, what are we going to do about it?'

There was silence and then David said: 'You heard me promise Rose that nothing would be done.'

'You were blackmailed into giving that promise. I don't take it seriously. If you let it drop it would be a sin, and Rose in after years when she has more sense might be the first to blame you. Anyway, I won't let you do it. If necessary, I will memorize the play or at least some of the best scenes and myself send them to Graham Bernard. I could probably get enough of it down on paper to interest him.'

'How wonderful you are,' said David.

'Wonderfully obstinate; but I do feel confident about this. It's not just because you are you that I'm so determined.'

'You don't need to tell me that.'

'Oh, don't be so humble! Of course there's the personal angle as well. I like you and you've got yourself caught up in a kind of thicket. My relations have the best intentions, but they have captured you, and they won't let you go if they can help it.'

'I dare say they would feel differently about it, if I made a big success – but shall I?'

'Nobody can be sure. In the past a few fine plays have failed, but only a few, and there's everything in your play to make it a success. Give it to me, please, David, and let me send it to Graham Bernard.'

'But what on earth shall I say to Rose?'

There was a slight coldness in Pearl's voice as she replied: 'That you must decide for yourself.'

'You think I'm terribly weak.'

'Only over her, and it's natural. It *is* horrid to have to hurt her; to have her weeping and wailing, and all the family wrangling about it.'

'I needn't tell her until I know something definite, and if Bernard turns it down I need never tell her,' said David.

'Don't talk as though you hope that's what he will do. All the opposition will mean nothing to you, if you have his assurance that I'm right. Then you will be bound to go ahead.'

David sighed : 'If only Rose could be pleased about it.'

'Yes, it's a shame, but I expect in the end she will be. May I have the play?'

'I've told you there's a copy in the desk.'

Pearl rose, opened the desk, and saw the neatly typed copy. David told her there should be some big envelopes in one of the drawers, and she found these, put the script into one of them, and tucked it under her arm. 'Well, now I've got my own way, I'd better be going,' she said, smiling at him. 'I was warned by Mrs Reever not to tire you by staying too long and, as I told you, this wasn't really intended to be a social call.'

David took her hand as she came to the bedside and held it in both of his, as he said : 'It's difficult to express gratitude, but I *am* grateful. If anything does come of this, I shall always remember how much I owe to you.'

'You owe me nothing, but if you think you do, then you can do something for me by not giving in.'

'I won't – though it beats me why you should care one way or the other. I mean if a man's such a poltroon, even his work can't matter much to you, or I would think not.'

Pearl laughed, telling him that was most illogical reasoning. Some of the most heroic plays had probably been written by men who looked like white mice. Not that he did, she hastened to say, and concluded : 'It's partly because you think so little of yourself that I would like to see the whole world think a lot of you.'

'You're a darling,' said David softly.

His clasp on her hand was so firm that she had to tug it away, which she did, still laughing at him.

'Now make haste and get quite well,' she said.

'I wonder if we shall ever be able to talk like this again,' David spoke rather sadly. 'I mean so freely, and with such understanding.'

'If we ever do, it will be when Rose is more reasonable about your future career. Until that happens we had better avoid each other, or she may suspect that I have encouraged you to rebel. I own I find it hard to hold my peace when I hear her talking of your work as though it's no more than a self-indulgence.'

'Don't blame her, Pearl. She's been brought up to look at things so differently.'

'I'm not blaming her – yet,' Pearl answered, somewhat cryptically.

✳ CHAPTER 8 ✳

Once David was up and working again, he and Rose renewed their old love and companionship, but to David there was a subtle difference in their relationship, though Rose was unaware of it. Now he was constantly hoping for a glimpse of Pearl, but that did not happen frequently for the weather was good and Pearl was often out when he called for Rose.

She was an odd girl, Kate remarked indulgently, with a great liking for her own company. She would go off alone for long walks, take a boat out, absent herself for hours, and when she was in the house she was so quiet that one scarcely knew she was there. She was really very clever, thought Kate, for she read such deep books, scarcely ever a novel, but books on theology, history and travel. None the less, both Kate and Rose found her a good companion. They could chatter away by the hour, and Pearl would be interested, making the right remarks at the appropriate moment.

Actually, she was waiting with secret impatience for Graham Bernard's verdict on David's play. She had sent it to him with a letter which was a brief reply to many which he had sent her during the last months, and he acknowledged receipt of the script and had assured her he would read it as soon as possible.

Then one day the anxiously awaited letter arrived. It was brief, and to her surprise told her that Bernard was staying with friends for a few days at a town only half an hour's train journey from Brightwell. He would take a chance and call on her that very afternoon. He hoped she would be in, though he was giving her such short notice, wrote Graham Bernard, adding that the play she had sent him to read was most interesting.

Rapidly Pearl skimmed through the remainder of the letter, then realized that within half an hour she might expect its writer to be with her. This visit was a stroke of luck which she had not expected. At the best she had hoped Bernard would write suggesting that David should come up to London and see him, though that would have meant conflict with his father and Rose, before anything definite was decided. But now, as he would be present, she could discover exactly what prospects of success there were, and David himself need not be involved until a later stage.

She avoided analysing her motives, though she knew these were only altruistic up to a point.

Going into the kitchen she returned with a lace afternoon cloth which she spread on the table. She took cups and saucers from the sideboard and set these out. Kate would soon be returning, for she had been out the greater part of the day, helping a friend who was moving from Northpond to settle in a nearby house.

Presently, while still occupied with her preparations, Pearl heard voices; Kate's voice, and also that of another woman. That meant Kate had brought Mrs Ford back with her for a cup of tea, which was only what might have been expected. Graham would drop in upon a family party, and how in the world was she to get him alone? Probably the only thing would be to take him round the garden on a tour of inspection.

In spite of the conflict in her mind, her manner was as calm and assured as usual when Kate came in accompanied by her friend whom Pearl had met casually a week or so before.

Mrs Ford, the wife of a prosperous draper, was not the type

of woman to interest Pearl under any circumstances, and today, untidy and exhausted with the effort of moving into a new home she was at her worst. She was a younger woman than Kate, probably in her middle thirties, the kind to be described as smart, since she slavishly followed the fashion trends. Her two children, both boys, were at boarding school.

In a parrot-like way she was a pretty woman; the sharp eyes and beaky nose being atoned for by a good complexion and teeth, and a head of luxuriant auburn hair. Her figure was also good, and her legs shapely.

'So there you are, dear,' said Kate with evident pleasure. 'I hoped you might be in. Oh, you're getting the tea. Well, I must say it will be welcome.'

Mrs Ford greeted Pearl affably. 'You look so cool and fresh as a daisy,' she said. 'Lucky you! Me, I've had quite a day of it. I don't know what I'd have done without Mrs Shandon. Moving's an exhausting business – men don't realize. The removal people were late getting here, but my hubby will come home this evening and expect to find everything ship-shape.'

'And so he will, or as near as makes no matter,' said Kate cheerfully. 'You've got the worst over. Sit down, dear, and put your feet up.'

With a sigh of relief Mrs Ford sank upon the sofa, but she said : 'I'm not feeling so bad, thanks to you, and after a cup of tea I shall be fine.'

'Well, Pearl's getting that ready as you can see, and you needn't worry about your evening meal. You and Mr Ford can come here for that. Shall I give you a hand, Pearl, or can you manage?'

Pearl smiled upon them both. 'Everything's ready. I cut sandwiches earlier. Sit down, and leave it to me.'

'I think we'd better have a snack on our own this evening,' said Mrs Ford, as Pearl disappeared into the kitchen. 'You know what men are. If my Tom gets talking to your husband, we shall never get a move on, and I want him to hang the curtains and the pictures.'

'Just as you like, dear,' said Kate, sitting down at the table as Pearl brought in the tea-pot. Smiling up at her step-daughter she said : 'I hope you've made it strong?' And she

60

stirred the contents of the pot with her teaspoon.

'You could walk on it as people say here.'

Mrs Ford looked at Pearl, taking in all the details of her appearance. Curiosity mingled with her approval. She said : 'It's nice for you to have a daughter at home, Mrs Shandon.'

'That's what I often say,' Kate agreed, 'though of course Rose is here and very helpful at weekends, and she gets home for her evening meal each day.'

'And when she marries, she will still be living quite near. You're lucky.'

'I certainly am.' Kate cast her eyes over the table and said with some surprise. 'Pearl dear, you have put cups and saucers for four.'

'An old friend rang me up a few minutes ago,' Pearl explained as she took a cup of tea over to Mrs Ford, and then proferred a plate of bread and butter. 'He has been staying with friends at Procanster, and is on his way back to London. But he decided to break his journey at Brightwell, and then catch a later train in order to see me.'

'How nice, dear,' said Kate with interest.

'I said I would give him a cup of tea. He'll have no time for that, though he says he can't stay long.'

'Shall we wait for him?' asked Kate.

'Oh no, it will take him a little time to get here, and you both look tired.'

'Well, I must say I'm gasping, and so is Mrs Ford. Anyway we can make fresh tea when he arrives.'

Mrs Ford remarked that Pearl must miss her London friends, to which Pearl replied vaguely that she hadn't had so many friends of late years.

'Pearl was nursing my husband's sister for a long time before she died,' Kate explained. 'She had a lingering illness, poor soul. It was a strain on Pearl, and after Cynthia died she was quite worn out and glad to come home for a rest and quiet.'

Mr Ford sighed : 'It's quite enough here for anyone. Tom has been set on this place for years, and when he knew Sunaglow was for sale, nothing would do for him but to make a bid for it. It's very healthy for the children when they come home for the holidays and fine for Tom with the golf course and all, but I don't know . . . I must say I like the shops.'

'You'll soon settle down,' Kate assured her. 'New villas are springing up all over the place, and the High Street shops are not too bad. It will be Northpond-by-the-Sea before we know where we are.'

'I felt better about it when I realized we'd be neighbours,' said Mrs Ford.

'Plenty of nice people have settled here already,' Kate said in her cheerful way. 'We're handy to the church, too, and the minister is popular and go-ahead. We're to have a dance at the parish hall next week, and they've started to get up an amateur dramatic club.'

Pearl sat listening to the conversation, glancing often at the clock, and presently she said : 'Kate, I think I'd better change my dress before my friend arrives. This one is only fit for the tub.'

Kate acquiesced, and when Pearl had left them, Mrs Ford said : 'What a nice looking girl she is.'

'Yes, she favours her father,' Kate agreed. 'More tea, dear?'

'If you would just add some to this.' Mrs Ford passed her cup. 'No more milk, please, I can't have it too strong. And then I'd better be away to the shops, and see what I can get for Tom's supper.'

'You'll find them very obliging,' Kate said. 'O'Leary, the grocer, is a great admirer of Pearl's, and sees we get our share of everything that's going. I'll tell her to put in a word for you.'

'I suppose she has all the local young men dangling after her?'

'They would be if they got any encouragement.'

'Stand-offish, is she?'

Kate answered after consideration : 'I wouldn't say that. It's more that she doesn't seem to notice them. She's a very quiet girl – good in the house, and does beautiful needlework, and reads a lot.'

'It's nice that she's settled down with you.'

'Yes, we are all glad to have her. She has the means though to live where she pleases. My sister-in-law left her well provided for.'

Mrs Ford, who took what she called a healthy interest in

the affairs of her friends – though the friends themselves had been known to describe it as unbearable curiosity – remarked that a girl with Pearl's looks was almost sure to marry, especially since she had money. This young man who was calling on her today, did Kate suppose there was anything in it?

There might be, Kate said, though he might not be a young man. Pearl hadn't said. She had even forgotten to mention his name.

Mrs Ford remarked after a pause : 'She doesn't look Spanish, or what you'd call foreign. Does she speak the language?'

'Not as far as I know,' replied Kate. 'Why should she, after all? She has never set foot in Spain.'

'But that's what her mother was?'

'A Spanish lady – yes.'

'Were there no relations on that side to take an interest in the girl?'

Kate, though wearying of the subject, answered civilly that Pearl's mother had been an only child; that she came of an aristocratic family who had died out. Pearl's mother, as Mrs Ford had probably heard, had herself died when the child was born, after not quite a year of marriage. Kate had known all about it at the time when she became engaged to Pearl's father, but it was all so long ago that they rarely spoke of it now.

'Well, I must say I should have wanted to know all the ins and outs of it,' Mrs Ford confessed. 'It's queer to think of such a steady-going man as your husband marrying abroad, and a foreigner, but then, he was young and romantic at that time. Of course there's been talk, about the girl coming to live with you; out of the blue as you might say, nobody having heard of her before.'

Kate bit back the retort that it was a pity people couldn't mind their own business. It wasn't the first time though that she had been questioned about Pearl, and she thought tolerantly that it was natural. She also would have been curious had any of her friends unexpectedly announced the arrival of an unknown step-daughter. Of course there were still a few left who remembered the child Pearl who had caused so much trouble, but that was years ago, and it so happened that since then they had moved from the neighbourhood.

'Pearl did stay with us for a time,' Kate explained, 'but my sister-in-law was very attached to her poor mother, and Pearl was at school in London, and well – it just happened that she stayed on and on with her.'

Mrs Ford said reflectively: 'You'd expect a girl who was half Spanish to be different somehow – more fire. I mean when one speaks of Spain one thinks of castanets and so on.'

Kate broke into a hearty laugh: 'Well, I must say I'm thankful Pearl doesn't go round the place clicking those things.'

Mrs Ford glanced at the clock and remarked that it was about time she made a move.

'If you want to get down to the shops, I could be setting your scullery to rights,' Kate offered.

This suggestion was accepted with suitable gratitude and suitable hesitation. 'Oh, would you? But I don't like to let you . . .'

'It's a pleasure. I was delighted when I heard you were coming to live so close to us. After all we saw a lot of each other when we lived in Northpond.'

The sound of a carriage drawing up outside attracted the attention of both women, and Mrs Ford went to the window and peeped out, cautiously standing behind the curtain, not to be seen.

'That's Pearl's friend now, I wouldn't wonder,' she said. 'It's the station cab. Yes, he's coming up the path. He's not what you would call young exactly – forty if he's a day. Smart looking man though.'

'I'll open the door,' said Kate, and went out to do so.

Mrs Ford took her compact from her bag and powdered her nose, gazing at herself critically in the tiny mirror. She didn't look too bad, she thought, in spite of her strenuous activities during the day. Out in the hall, Kate was welcoming the visitor, whom she then ushered into the room, saying as she did so: 'I'll tell Pearl you're here.'

Mrs Ford studied the guest with interest. Very good-looking, what you might call distinguished, but certainly forty, if not older. She approved of his height, his pleasant,

64

rough-hewn face, and his clothes which were evidently the product of a first-class tailor and worn with ease.

'This is our neighbour, Mrs Ford,' said Kate. 'At least she will be. She's just moving in, and I'm giving her a hand. Pearl said she would have a friend calling on his way to London, but she forgot to tell me the name.'

'It's Graham Bernard,' said the visitor with a pleasant smile for Mrs Ford who murmured : 'How do you do,' in a vague and fluttery way.

Kate said : 'The name sounds familiar. I'm sure I've heard Pearl speak of you.'

'It would be nice to think she had,' Bernard responded. 'Her aunt was a very old friend of mine. A wonderful woman.'

'Oh, she was, and she suffered so much,' Kate sighed. 'It was really a merciful release; that's what I told Pearl when she first came home, though she was very cut up, poor girl. She was devoted to Cynthia.'

Graham Bernard agreed. He remarked that he had seen a good deal of Cynthia Shandon during her years of illness, and Pearl had been wonderful – capable and completely selfless. He sat down in one of the big armchairs, and when Kate said she would put the kettle on so that Pearl could make fresh tea for him, he checked her.

'Please don't trouble,' he said, 'I had tea before I left Procanster. What a charming part of the world this is. London by contrast seems very dark and dull.'

'Oh, I wouldn't live there for anything,' Mrs Ford assured him earnestly.

He started to talk about the neighbourhood and all the amenities, and Kate breathed a sigh of relief, thankful that the other woman was there. She knew only too well that entertaining strangers was not her forte.

Pearl entered the living-room to find Mrs Ford monopolizing the conversation, while Bernard sat back in his easy chair, listening to her with a polite smile. Kate sat stiffly upright, with her hands folded in her lap, and evinced relief when she saw Pearl. Bernard rose to shake hands with her, and gazed at her with approval : 'You look much better than when I last saw you,' he said.

Smiling benevolently upon them, Kate told him that they

all noticed the difference, for Pearl had been only skin and bone four months ago.

'It seems longer than four months,' said Bernard. 'You have been missed, Pearl. When are you coming back?'

'Oh, not for a long time yet,' Kate protested. 'It's far better for her here than life in London, and we should find it hard to part with her, even for a visit.'

Mrs Ford, glancing once more at the clock, said deprecatingly that she was afraid she must be going, and Kate at once assured her that she was ready to accompany her. Apologizing to Bernard she said: 'Forgive me for rushing off, but you know how it is when a house is upside down. The rooms at Mrs Ford's new home must be got into some sort of shape, so that she and her husband can sleep there tonight. Anyway, you two must have a lot to talk about, and Pearl said you couldn't stay long.'

Bernard replied that he was on his way to London, and wanted to get there that night, however late it might be, as he had important business to transact the next day; whereupon, Kate putting out her hand bade him goodbye and remarked that she hoped she might have the pleasure of meeting him again. Any friend of Pearl's was warmly welcome.

Bernard thanked her and Mrs Ford, following Kate out of the room, said sportively that it was certainly a case of Hail and Farewell!

Pearl laughed as the door closed upon them, for Bernard's expression struck her as comical. 'She's a curiosity of a woman, really not typical,' she said. 'It's luck they left us alone though. I hardly dared hope they would. Sit down, Graham—do. Don't you really want any tea?'

'No, really. I had a whisky just before I arrived.'

'I'm sorry I can't offer you another, but we're strictly teetotal here, and tea is our perpetual stand-by.'

'Good lord!'

Bernard looked round the room and then looked at Pearl, recalling the charm and taste of Cynthia Shandon's London home. In such a setting as this, Pearl was distinctly out of place, though there was no denying that she bloomed with health, looking better than he had ever seen her. He said: 'You might say you are pleased to see me.'

66

'I am. It's like a breath of fresh air.'

'I should think you get enough of that, if nothing else,' and he glanced out of the window upon the neat garden and the smooth stretch of sea.

Pearl well knew what was passing through his mind, and she had to laugh. Dear Graham who thought of the country and the seaside as places to avoid if it was humanly possible. He must certainly be puzzled. 'Brightwell,' she said, 'is an extremely healthy place.'

'Why on earth have you buried yourself here?'

'You heard what my step-mother said, and it's true. I was a wreck when I first came here.'

'Yes – well, you had a wretched time; poor, dear Cynthia. I hope she acted fairly by you, Pearl.'

'More than fairly. She left me everything. I've nothing to worry about over money. One day I may return to live in the London house, and there's the cottage in Sussex as well. At the moment they are closed up. I've made no plans about them. The only thing I wanted was to get away from it all.'

'But that was four months ago,' Bernard remonstrated, 'and even then, surely Italy or the South of France would have suited you better than this place? You have so many friends – several of them would have gone with you. Ellen Vincey for one. She's devoted to you.'

'I know – dear Ellen, but it happened that at the time Aunt Cynthia died I was in one of my periodical throes of longing for a home, and people of my own.'

'But that good soul I've just met. Really . . .'

Pearl said thoughtfully : 'There's something very comforting about Kate. You were out of London when Aunt Cynthia died, but she and Father came up for the funeral and the memorial service. She was so kind to me. She made me feel I was really wanted. She hasn't an idea in her head beyond her home and her family and the church, but even that seemed restful four months ago. Besides, there's my sister – and my father.'

Bernard looked at her keenly, wondering about her, as he had wondered many a time before. 'I heard all about that from Cynthia, it was an everlasting mystery to her.'

'Yes, I know. She did her best to talk me out of it. She

never understood Father, and they didn't get on very well.'

'Cynthia said your father was a weak, dull man, who had no interests outside his business.'

'That,' said Pearl without rancour, 'is a fairly accurate description.'

'You're disillusioned then?'

Pearl sighed and was silent for a short space, leaning back in her chair, her eyes dreamy. She said at last: 'I never had any illusions about my father, but it made no difference. I wanted to be with him. All through my childhood it was the unattainable goal.'

'How do you feel about it now?' Bernard asked.

'Oh, pretty dead, I suppose. And yet – even now, I keep thinking, keep wondering . . . what was there in him that made my mother so adore him? She lived for him, and when she knew he was cooling towards her, she was glad to die. Aunt Cynthia would talk about it for hours. She thought it the most extraordinary romance.'

It did not seem particularly extraordinary to Bernard and he said so. Miles Shandon from all accounts had been a good-looking chap, the kind to throw a girl off her balance through physical attraction.

'I think my mother must have seen more in him than that,' said Pearl. 'Something noble or spiritual. Perhaps something of what she felt was transmitted to me. At one time though I so seldom saw him, he was the only man who mattered in the least to me.'

'At one time! Has anyone else cropped up?'

'No. I only mean that although I thought it impossible I'm cured of my infatuation. I can do without him now.'

'Then,' said Bernard with satisfaction, 'there's nothing to prevent you from coming back to London and marrying me.'

Pearl looked at him with a softened expression. Was this the fifth or sixth time he had asked her to marry him? She could not remember. And at least he was aware of her origin. Most people who knew Graham Bernard said he was hard to an abnormal degree, but Pearl had seen a different side to his character.

'I've never understood why you want to marry me,' she said.

'There's my heritage. Marriage would be more than a normal risk.'

Bernard made an impatient gesture. 'My dear girl,' he said, 'your mother was a Hindu lady of illustrious descent. That sounds good enough to me. My own beginnings were pretty humble; my father, as I've told you, was a night porter at a far from exclusive hotel. But what does it matter who or what our parents were? You are no snob, and I have no racial prejudices.'

'What about possible progeny?' Pearl asked flippantly.

He looked at her, appraised her cool, unusual beauty, and smiled. 'They would be proud and beautiful, as you are.'

How could she not like him and be grateful . . .? A hard man, a superb business man who had fought his way to the top, a man with many enemies, many satellites, few real friends, who yet was possessed of so much chivalry and goodness. She said : 'I shall never marry, but perhaps – something less binding.'

He gazed at her in astonishment. 'What a strange girl you are. I can offer you a good deal, you know.'

'Yes, but marriage is too high a price.'

Bernard laughed : 'It's usually the man who thinks that.'

'Oh Graham,' Pearl said impatiently, 'don't pretend I'm talking nonsense. Of course several men have made passes at me, but few of them would consider marrying me. I don't blame them. My grandmother was a Maharanee, but she lived in purdah all her life.'

'But what on earth does it matter?' asked Bernard. 'There's a lot of nonsense talked about the gulf between East and West. You have never known your mother's country or your mother's people. You are English. So am I, though my mother was a Jewess. Do you find that objectionable?'

'Of course not.'

'All the talk about the races not intermingling is absurd – they do mingle. There must be an astronomical amount of Americans with a touch of dark blood, and they're none the worse for it.'

'I know – of course I know, we've talked of it before, but not today, Graham. We haven't too much time, and I

69

want to hear what you think of the play I sent you.'

'It's promising. I told you so in my letter.'

'Sufficiently promising for you to promote it?'

'I haven't made up my mind. It's witty and clever, but it needs more action.'

'But David could write that in,' said Pearl eagerly. 'I could make him see what you wanted.'

That was undoubtedly true. In the matter of construction she could help him, and how pleasant that would be, if only Rose and the family would be reasonable about it; pleased at his chance of success.

'I believe in this play,' she said earnestly. 'I've a feeling about it. You used to trust my judgement, Graham. Remember how I urged you to risk *Youth's Manuscript*, when you were doubtful about it?'

'You have a certain flair,' Bernard admitted.

'Yes, I have.' Her voice was confident.

Bernard looked at her keenly: 'This man who wrote it. What is he to you?'

'I've told you. My sister is engaged to him.'

'And are you so attached to her?'

Pearl shrugged, said indifferently: 'I'm quite fond of Rose.'

'Fond!' Bernard uttered a short laugh. 'That's a word not in your vocabulary. It's either love or hate with you.'

He knew her too well, thought Pearl; probably because in some ways they resembled each other. With a disarming lightness, she said: 'Rubbish! I've been mildly fond of many people.'

'But you didn't go out of your way for them. About this play, you have been eager; so much so that you got in touch with me, answered one of my many letters.'

Pearl admitted to herself that she had been stupidly neglectful. Bernard was a valuable friend and should not have been ignored· for months on end. But since leaving London, she had scarcely written to a soul. At first she had been too ill and wretched, and later she had been possessed by that futile longing to be drawn into the home circle, absorbed in it, accepted by it, and all because of her tortuous, tormented love for Miles.

'I should have written sooner or later,' she said.

'Much later, probably. I'm sorry to seem sceptical, but few women are disinterested; few men either. If I do put on this play, what is there in it for me?'

'Success, money, additional prestige,' Pearl suggested.

'Not sufficient. I want you back in London.'

'I've said I won't marry you.'

'But you hinted at an alternative. Oh, I know you're making no promises, and I don't want you as a mistress. I never have done. I'd rather have your companionship and friendship, with the hope that one day you'll marry me. Even the comradeship of shared work means a lot to me.'

He was a fine person, Pearl thought. She understood him and could sympathize, but apart from that there was nothing. Unfortunately one rarely loved a man for his qualities.

Suddenly Bernard made up his mind. It was often so. He had faith in his snap decisions: 'I'll do something about this play,' he said, 'if it's only a trial run at the Lester; but not unless you are on the spot. I've missed you. Why do you think I called day after day to see Cynthia, right to the last, if it was not for you?'

'You had been friendly with her for years,' Pearl reminded him.

'Yes, for at one time she was a vital, stimulating woman; she had a tremendous sense of humour, but latterly, after her second stroke, it could have been no pleasure to anyone to visit her frequently. It was tragic even to look at her. I wonder how you endured it.'

'She loved me,' said Pearl, 'and I still loved her, even when she was too lost to know I did.'

Bernard saw that she was now very pale. He had switched her mind back to the past, and looking at her he realized how intensely she must have suffered. Yet in Cynthia Shandon's home, even at the last, there had been brightness. Pearl had willingly isolated herself; there had never been a parade of sacrifice. Once Bernard had heard her say, as she bent over the helpless woman: 'I want to be with you. I need to be with you.' No doubt she had said it dozens of times, in that soft voice, when he had not been there. Cynthia had always loved her, but that love must have approached adoration during the last years of her life, for her mind had been clear enough, poor soul, though she could not move and was al-

71

most speechless. Pearl was wrong in saying that Cynthia had been too ill to realize the great reward which her goodness to a desolate child had reaped. Yet as he well knew there was another side to her character. A cold ruthlessness, an indifference to suffering as it affected those who meant nothing to her. In the early stages of her aunt's illness, she had dismissed a maid who had been with her for years, and for nothing except that the woman's fussy affection played on the invalid's nerves. Old Amy's abject plea to be allowed to stay, her tears and her grief, had not moved Pearl in the slightest. She had been sent off with a money present which had done little to compensate her for the separation. There had been men, too; Pearl liked to be admired and she could be teasingly sweet and cruel. It was all a game to her; a game of power, and she cared nothing for the suffering she was inflicting.

'You're a strange mixture,' he said.

'Aren't we all?' she retorted, and then after a pause she said : 'Very well, Graham, I will come back to London for a few weeks anyway, if you promise to put on the play at the Lester.'

'And if it goes further – to the Corinthian?'

'We can talk about that later.'

'Don't think I'm stuck for a play,' said Bernard. 'I've an option on half a dozen.'

Pearl smiled and said : 'You always have.'

'And don't think I'm deceived. You're not making this effort only because David Page is your sister's young man.'

He was too shrewd for her, Pearl realized, but she could not confide in him, could not explain that so far as David was concerned, she hoped for nothing. There was her stern sense of obligation towards Rose. She would never compete with her, for she had done her sufficient injury in the past. Nevertheless, she would not, if she could help it, allow David to be sacrificed – not to the extent of his whole future. She said : 'Suppose for argument's sake that I do – like him?'

'Just the same I'd want you back, if only to have you around. Also, I'm a patient man – I can wait.'

Wait, Pearl supposed, until what he considered a fervent, physical passion had worn itself out. Unable to share his conviction that in the end she would settle for a union based on mutual tastes and understanding, she still could not entirely dismiss such a possibility.

It might happen – it could happen – one day when she was tired of loneliness; weary of herself, and longing for understanding.

In silence they considered each other, and in that silence the front door was heard to open and close, and to Pearl's astonishment and concern, she heard Rose's voice. The time had slipped away, and they had not noticed it.

❋ CHAPTER 9 ❋

Rose came out of the school gates to find David waiting for her. She was popular with her students and had a teenage girl hanging on to each of her arms. One carried her books, and both were chattering animatedly to her. But when they saw David the chattering ceased, and they stared at him with mingled curiosity and bashfulness. Everyone at the school knew that Rose was engaged. They admired her sapphire ring and her good looks, and she was romantic to them. Motor cars also were still a novelty, and to drive in one was wonderful.

Now the two girls escorting her were thrilled to have a glimpse of David. She was sufficiently near them in age to have a good idea of what was passing in their minds, and was amused; but she was also sympathetic, and she introduced both girls to David by name, and he shook hands with them.

'I got off a bit earlier today, so I thought I might as well drive you home,' he said. Rose replied that that was a good idea. She got into the car while the two girls stood with linked arms, watching them and giggling a little.

'Odd to think that a few years ago I was just like they are,' said Rose, as after a few preliminary grunts from the motor they drove off.

'You don't look much older now.' David patted her knee affectionately. 'I thought we might go to the pictures this evening. There's that one about the navy on at the Royal. I hear it's good.'

'That would be lovely.'

'Shall we go out for a meal first? We can drop in and tell your mother.'

'She may not be at home. She was to help that tiresome Mrs Ford to move in today, and she may be kept at it for hours. Pearl will be in though, I expect, and even if she's not, I can leave a note.'

'Yes; you can say that we've gone off for the evening.'

'I wish I could think we were going off together, not to come back.' A note of wistful sadness was in her voice.

David looked at her with surprise, with a lurking hope. 'Do you? Away from Brightwell for ever?'

'Of course not. I was thinking of our honeymoon. We'd come back after a few weeks, but it would be to our own home. Everything would be settled. We should be sure of each other.'

David looked straight ahead as he drove. For a moment he had hoped, but he should have known Rose better. He said : 'We're sure of each other now.'

'It's not the same thing, is it? Sometimes I feel as though the whole world is trying to crowd in between us, to separate us. I even imagine you are being kind to me deliberately, taking pains about it, and not finding it easy.'

'Rose, that's complete nonsense,' David expostulated.

Rose glanced at him, and then she smiled : 'Yes, I expect it is, really.'

'You're a goose.' David stopped before the house. 'Now run along in, and if there's nobody at home, write your note explaining.'

'Come with me. I want you to kiss me, and you can't here, with people passing.'

David laughed, and followed her up the garden path. Rose fitted her key in the lock and went in, calling aloud in the hall : 'Is anyone at home?'

Almost instantly the living-room door opened and Pearl appeared. She said : 'Kate is out, but I'm here. Aren't you early?'

'Yes, because David called for me and drove me home.'

Rose walked into the living-room and saw Bernard. In the

74

hall, Pearl and David exchanged a speechless glance before they followed her. Rose, taken by surprise, stared at Bernard and then said : 'Oh, I'm sorry. I didn't know.'

Pearl intervened. She said : 'Rose, this is Graham Bernard. He called to see me on his way to London. Graham, this is my sister and her fiancé.'

Rose said in some confusion : 'We noticed the station cab, but I thought it must be for someone calling at The Pines. That's the house next but one to this.' In a different voice she asked : 'What's the matter, David?' for he was gazing at Graham Bernard with incredulity, and a touch of awed excitement. He murmured : 'Graham Bernard !'

His tone was so strange that Rose was bewildered, but only for a minute, then the implication of the name dawned upon her, and she involuntarily gasped, as Pearl, aware that Rose could be unpredictable and fearing a scene, said quickly : 'David, I'm glad you came in. Graham has to get the London train, that's why the cab is waiting, and there seemed little chance you would be able to meet him today.'

'What brought him here?' Rose said, and then instantly apologized : 'I beg your pardon. I didn't mean . . . of course you and Pearl are old friends and it was natural for you to break your journey to see her.'

Bernard looked at her curiously, suspecting conflict, but uncertain of its cause. He said : 'I wanted to see your sister – to find out how she was. She's been a long time away from all her London friends.'

'Yes, she has,' Rose agreed.

'And there was also this play she sent me to read.'

Rose's gaze moved from David to Pearl, while her face paled. She said incredulously : 'You sent it to him, Pearl?'

'Is it any good?' David asked eagerly.

How well Bernard knew that look of mingled hope and excitement, but it never failed to touch him. He said : 'Weren't you persuaded of it by your local success?'

'No.' David smiled and shook his head.

'Very sensible of you.'

'Then you're not – not impressed?' Rose said, her eyes fixed on Bernard.

'On the contrary, I'm prepared to take an option on it.'

75

Pearl interposed : 'Not an option, Graham.'

Leaning negligently against a chair, she was smiling, and he grinned ruefully correcting himself, saying : 'What I mean is this. I'm prepared to put it on for a try-out at a London suburban theatre of which I am a director. If it does well there, if it is favourably received by the press and the audience, it may go further. We shall see. I promise to do my best for you.'

David thought the words so incredible that he would have been glad to have heard them repeated, not once but half a dozen times. Then they might have fully convinced him.

'That's marvellous,' he said in a dazed voice. 'I don't know how to thank you.'

Bernard glanced from the sullen-browed Rose to David's eager face. The chap was attractive, he thought regretfully; the type who might well catch a woman's fancy. He had brains too, and imagination. He felt a passing pity for Rose. If Pearl had set her heart on David there was little hope for her, poor, commonplace child.

'Thank your advocate here. She's a very persuasive one,' he said, with his hand on Pearl's arm.

She said : 'I could have persuaded you for ages, and it would have been useless had the play not appealed to you.'

'Well, yes, that's true,' he agreed. 'Come and see me off, my dear. I can't delay any longer. Good afternoon, Miss Shandon. Page, I shall be seeing you in London, later on.'

Pearl went with Bernard to the gate. 'Dear Graham, I'm truly grateful,' she said.

'Do you plan to split up that affair?' he asked abruptly, looking keenly at her.

'No. How horrible you must think me. They're in love, and they'll be happy – but in David's way, or I hope so.'

Bernard shook a puzzled head. He said : 'I shall never understand women, but it's no affair of mine. What concerns me is your promise to return to London.'

'I shall keep it. I shall want to, once rehearsals start. It will be so exciting.'

'And you and I will have good times – go out together as we used to.'

'We will.'

'That's enough to be going on with. In the future – well, we shall see.'

He stooped to kiss her cheek before he got into the cab. She stood at the gate, watching as he was driven away.

Meanwhile, David faced a Rose he scarcely recognized. 'You – you, how could you, David?' Her eyes were dilated with anger. He said, still caught up in his dream : 'It's the most incredible luck.'

'You promised me; you promised Daddy,' Rose cried.

Reluctantly David returned to reality, to the passionate and unhappy girl to whom he was pledged; to the ordinary considerations of life. He said soberly : 'Yes – so I did. I'm sorry, Rose.'

'Sorry! Is that all you have to say?'

'Yes. I *am* sorry – for you. I realize how it must seem to you.'

With a wild reproach, Rose cried : 'You deceived me, you lied to me, you went behind my back and so did Pearl. I shall never trust either of you again.'

The elation was still in David's eyes, even his concern for Rose could not quench it; and it was not an unalloyed concern; there was also resentment. 'Your terms were too hard,' he said.

'I don't understand.'

'You've got to understand. It's my work. I've laboured at it for months – it means a lot to me. The chance Pearl offered me was too good to lose. I was afraid to hope anything would come of it, but I had to take it.'

'But I told you what it would mean to me if you did take it,' Rose protested.

'Yes – you put the screw on me.'

She stared at him. This couldn't be David, using a rough voice to her, looking at her as though she were a stranger, as though her wishes and her unhappiness mattered nothing to him. 'What a beastly thing to say,' she stormed.

Pearl re-entered the room as Rose's protest rang out. She stood looking at her with a pity which was greater than David's. 'I wanted you to meet Graham,' she said, 'and yet I'm sorry you came back. It's so hard on Rose.'

Rose flashed her an angry glance. She had loved Pearl.

She had been proud of her; admired and trusted her, and Pearl had made a fool of her. 'Much you care about me,' she said bitterly.

'I do care.' Pearl's voice was grave and low. 'I would spare you unhappiness if I could.'

Rose began to tremble. She had to clench her hands to force her voice to steadiness: 'You treacherous, you . . .' she began, and broke off, gasping.

David took her arm and shook it. 'Stop it, Rose. Stop it I say,' he commanded.

Rose pressed her hands against her mouth. She was suddenly frightened by her own intensity, by the words which had sprung to her lips to hurl at her sister. There was hate in her heart, and a wild desire to hurt Pearl as she had been hurt. But she was powerless. Pearl was strong and ruthless, and she would not care.

'You would have had to know,' Pearl said, 'but David or I could have broken it to you, could possibly have made you see everything in a different light.'

'Never.'

'But it's fantastic. Most girls would be proud and happy.'

'Happy to be deceived?' Rose asked bitterly.

'No, not that, though we were forced into it. David hated that part of it. He would have told you, I think, if he could have been sure that Graham would be impressed by the play, but he knew you would make a scene, and shirked risking one for an uncertainty.'

They were leagued against her, thought Rose, and knew a frantic sense of helplessness, of being trapped. They were wrecking her whole life and they did not care. She saw all her plans and hopes and her entire neat future which had seemed so secure, falling in chaos around her.

'How you have plotted and schemed,' she said bitingly. 'You must have talked me over and criticized me. I can imagine it — so patronizingly kind and sorry for me; telling yourselves it wasn't my fault I was so narrow in my ideas, though it was a pity. You despise all I stand for, and all I value.'

Pearl, listening to this outcry, knew that Rose would never believe she was sorry for her. Rose could only love and understand according to a pattern. She had her own code which she would follow. If she made a promise she would keep it, and she expected the same of David.

'To be truthful we have scarcely mentioned you,' said Pearl. 'I told David I would send the play to Graham with my recommendation, if he could nerve himself to withstand the family wrath, and then he made up his mind and gave me the play. That's all there is to it.'

'It's enough too,' said Rose.

But now David was fully aware of her suffering, and his pleasure and sense of achievement were dimmed. She was pitiful to him, his poor little Rose. He said : 'Oh, my dear, I'm sorry to have hurt you, but I couldn't help it.'

His arm was round her, and briefly she allowed him to hold her, but then she pushed him away from her. 'You're so weak,' she said angrily. 'I've tried my utmost to build you up. I've pleaded with you to work. I made Daddy believe in you. He wanted us not to be engaged until you were further advanced, but I wore him down. You would never have had the promise of a partnership but for me. You think you owe a lot to yourself and to your writing, but you owe far more to me, to your father and mine, and to the factory.'

'Oh, curse the factory!' David cried. 'I'm sick to death of it.'

'David !'

Now she was aghast, for he had really shocked her, but the words could not be unsaid, and he had no intention of re-calling them. Let her for once, he thought, see things from his point of view; let her try to understand him, allow him his rights as a human being.

'It's true, Rose,' he said. 'I'm sorry, but it is. I'm not interested in textiles, what's more I'm bored with the everlasting, never-changing grind. I care precious little about money, and nothing at all for a commercial success. I want to get away, and the sooner the better.'

It was as though his words fell like stones into a pool of silence. Rose was rigid as she gazed at him. She said at last in a stricken voice : 'You don't love me.'

David went on doggedly : 'I want you to chuck all this – this obsession about building a house, and the necessity of a safe, prosperous existence. I want you to marry me and to come to London with me. I want you to take a chance.'

Rose was silent. She stared at him, and stared again.

'Why don't you, Rose?' Pearl asked gently.

'Why don't I what?' Rose spoke in a dazed voice, not looking at her.

'Take a chance. There's nothing to prevent you. You are of age. You can marry David long before the autumn and go to London with him. You can share everything with him; his success and his failures.'

'No,' said Rose flatly.

'Father is very soft with you. He would forgive you. He might even be proud of you, for your courage.'

Suddenly Rose seemed to come to life. She swung round and faced Pearl. There was defiance and hatred in her voice as she cried : 'I'll never do such a thing. But I won't give up David. He'll have to jilt me, he'll have to throw me over and shame me – and that he never will.'

Pearl shrugged wearily, with resignation. 'I'm quite sure he won't.'

'Don't think I'm blaming only him,' said Rose. 'I blame you far more. You're clever, Pearl; you're treacherous and stealthy. You talked David into all this. I was a fool to trust you.'

'Perhaps you were,' said Pearl in a sombre voice, and then she added : 'It's not my custom to interfere, but in this case I found I could not help it. I saw something fine being wasted, thrown away. I know it doesn't seem like that, to you, but I've been brought up in the theatre world, and I could see what was being done to David. You were too inexperienced to value his work; he was too modest and himself inexperienced. He only knew he loved it.'

'But it's no business of yours. It's my life – mine and David's, and you are destroying it. He would never have thought of such madness but for you.'

'That's just the point,' Pearl drily observed.

'We were happy,' Rose cried, her voice breaking. 'You may not believe it, but we were. Our engagement put everything right, for all of us, for David's father as well as for me, and for Daddy and Mummy. There's nobody else to carry on the family business, and for a time it seemed as though David wouldn't. But then when we loved each other, it was different. He saw what a fine thing it could be. He realized how we could work together, share all our interests, and bring up our children to follow in the same way. Everything was going well until you – until you . . .'

'Spoilt everything. Yes, I see that.'

'Then aren't you ashamed of being so cruel?'

'No, because I think that art, that genius and its natural expression are more important than commercialism.'

'But Mummy and I have been so fond of you. Mummy has been so good to you; she was sorry for you when you first came here, ill and wretched; she would have done anything for you. And I – I was glad when you came home. I thought Father had been terribly unjust to you; it always worried me. It's only now I see how right he was in wanting to keep you apart from me. When you threw that knife at me, you scarred my cheek. That I forgave, but this is different; it's much worse, and I'll never forgive you, not even in the last moment of my life.'

On the last words Rose broke. The tears which had been held back overwhelmed her, and she ran sobbing from the room.

Pearl made a movement as though to follow her, but then she checked herself. There was no reasoning with Rose now. She would have to calm down before one could hope to do any good with her.

David said : 'I'm sorry, Pearl.'

Pearl sighed : 'She's terribly upset.'

'What she said was true.' David's voice was stern.

'About me? That I'm stealthy, treacherous?'

'That's nonsense of course. What I mean is that Rose stumbled on the truth when she said I no longer loved her.'

'Don't, David!'

Involuntarily Pearl put out her hands. It was as though she tried to thrust away the inevitable. She hadn't wanted this – or had she? All she knew was that she had seen it coming nearer with every passionate, uncontrolled word Rose uttered.

'And Rose doesn't love me,' David went on steadily. 'Her one idea is to hold me – whether I love her, or whether I don't; whether we can be happy or as miserable as hell together.'

'If I had never come here,' Pearl brooded.

Her head was downbent, but she knew that David was nearer to her, that he was looking at her as she had known he could look – fully awakened, caught between pain and a tremendous glory.

'Don't regret that. Whatever happens, never regret that – promise me,' he said softly.

'Very well, I promise.'

There was no fighting the moment. It was part of the pattern – her pattern and David's . . . not Rose's. Later one might fight, because one owed Rose a debt which must be repaid. But now . . . now . . .

'Pearl!' David said.

There was that in his voice which could not be denied. She lifted her head as he pulled her into his arms.

※ CHAPTER 10 ※

Rose lay face downwards on her bed, but her tears were over. Tears were an expression of grief, and her state of mind was one of anger rather than sorrow. She heard David walk down the garden pathway; she heard him drive away. They were to have had a happy evening together, and now there was this. Presently Pearl knocked on the door. Rose's impulse was to be silent, then perhaps her sister would go away, but she hadn't locked the door, and after a few moments it opened.

'Rose, are you asleep?' Pearl asked.

Rose did not answer in words, but she got up from the bed and went across to the dressing-table. She sat down on the stool before the mirror and gazed at her tear-marked face. She was so pale that the scar on her cheek was more noticeable than usual. She wondered if Pearl saw that.

'Do listen to me,' said Pearl.

'As you're here, I can't help listening.'

'David has gone.'

'I know – I heard the motor.'

'There's so much I want to say, so much David couldn't say. It's quite natural you should hate me, and everything you said was natural, feeling as you do. But we're both intelligent and reasonable, and we're not children. Listen, Rose, this isn't the only kind of life in which you can be happy. You think so because you have no experience of any other.'

'That's not true. I'm no country bumpkin. I lived abroad for two years.'

'Yes – well, that isn't what I meant. You don't know anything about artistic success and how exciting it can be. It's true David may fail, but it isn't likely. Graham is a successful man, and he scarcely ever makes a mistake about a play. You would have a wonderful life in London, Rose.'

Rose turned on the dressing stool to face her. She said : 'You have no more understanding of my life, than I have of yours. I don't want that kind of life. I've told you so over and over again.'

'Doesn't David count at all with you – what he wants?'

'I know what's best for him. Everything you think worthwhile, I think false and unreal, and so would most sensible people. What I can't get over is the way you seem to think you have a right to interfere, to come between David and me.'

'It isn't interference. Rose, you are good at languages. Supposing you had a girl at your school who had a real talent for French or German, and her people objected to her learning because they wanted her to take up some domestic work, wouldn't you try to help her, wouldn't you put in a word for her?'

'I suppose I might,' Rose reluctantly agreed, 'but if very strong objections were raised, I should give it up. I should think I had no right to make trouble in her home. I dare say you would act differently. You would side with her, and ignore the wishes of the family. You might go behind their backs and help her secretly.'

'I probably would, because I hate to see people frustrated. Rose, you and David will never be happy unless you meet him half-way. Couldn't you take the long view? Even if he decides to refuse this partnership and give all his time to writing, you can look ahead to your children. Father is not an old man, neither is Mr Page, they might well carry on until they have grandsons to take their places.'

'That's too visionary for me. I want children of course, but

83

I might not have any.'

'David would always be grateful, if you stood by him now,' Pearl persisted.

'It doesn't follow. In a few years' time he might regret it terribly, and then he would wish I had not given in to his weakness. Why can't you leave us alone? You've done a lot of harm, but now it's up to David and me. It will be a fight, but I shall win.'

'Are you sure?'

For an instant Pearl saw fear flash across Rose's face, but then sullen gloom obscured all other expression. 'I shan't break off our engagement, and neither will he,' said Rose.

'I know that, but you can't force another human being to lead a life they hate. If you could only believe it, I'm as concerned for you – more concerned – than I am for him. I know it's partly through me you are unhappy, and I did enough injury in the past, as you have reminded me.'

Rose was silent. She took up her brush and attacked her curly hair with a vigour which partly dispersed her anger.

'If it's money that worries you, it needn't,' Pearl said. 'I have Aunt Cynthia's house. You could live there, both of you. I have money and I would share it with you, until David has made enough.'

Rose stared at her in amazement. 'You're extraordinary. How can you think I would accept so much, and why should you offer it?'

'Because I owe you so much by way of atonement. Don't you see, if you get your own way now you may be miserable all your life, and I must prevent that – if I can. Think what it will mean to be married to a man who has an everlasting grudge against you. What woman could bear it?'

Rose found it hard to doubt her sincerity. She said: 'I may as well speak my mind. I think you've been horribly sly and mischief-making, but – but perhaps I said too much just now. You may be fond of me in a way, and not want me to be parted from David, but you only see one side of him. Just now he's carried away, but we've been happy here, and we shall be happy again. Running away with him and marrying him may seem romantic to you, but to me it seems hateful. I should feel terrible and people would think – well, they might think anything. That I had cause to be ashamed perhaps. Besides I wouldn't upset Daddy and Mummy so much, and I won't let David disappoint everyone. At one time, Pearl, I hoped you would stay here for ages; for ever if you wanted to. But now I think it would be a mistake. If you go away I can make David see reason.'

. 'I shan't stay here indefinitely,' said Pearl.

Rose wanted to say that Pearl must go soon, must go now, but she could not utter the words. That was chiefly because she knew Pearl would only leave when she was ready to leave. Nothing anyone could say would make any difference.

By unspoken consent neither of the girls confided in Kate, or gave any open indication of distress. Nevertheless Kate was aware of tension.

Pearl had always been rather quiet, but now it was a different kind of quietness. Before, she had been attentive, and she had been amused when Rose chattered, but now she was withdrawn. It was as though she listened to a voice within herself, not to those around her.

And Rose no longer chattered gaily about trivialities. Often she would make an effort to seem bright, an effort which, so Kate suspected, was for her benefit. Was there some ·secret between the two girls? If so, it might be something quite harmless, some surprise they were planning, but it was difficult for her to believe it, for although Pearl and Rose were polite to each other, the old intimacy was lacking. Rose no longer teased and adored Pearl; Pearl no longer looked at Rose with that half-smile, watching her with tolerant pleasure, as one might watch an engaging child.

None of these half-suspicions were very clear to Kate; they floated hazily through her mind, bewilderingly tangled; but all that was sensitive in her responded to them. Now and again she would put a tentative question to Rose, who either evaded her or seemed not to understand. She went off to her work as usual, went out in the evenings with David as usual, but he came less often to the house.

Kate studied her daughter's face. She was pale and her eyes were shadowed; sometimes, when she believed herself to be unobserved, her lips would droop in a desolate fashion.

Pearl's face told Kate nothing. It was serene, gentle, as it had always been. A mask, thought Kate, with irrational irritation.

Pearl was often awake before her on these fine sunny mornings, and on one occasion Kate came upon her when her face was anything but mask-like. The postman had just left the letters and Pearl had collected them. There were two or three for her, and the rest she had put down on the hall table. One she had torn open and read, and for an instant Kate saw her face alive, quivering with some emotion, whether distress or joy she could not have said. She did notice that the letter was typewritten and then, as Pearl became aware of her, she crumpled the sheet of paper in her hand and smiled in her usual placid way.

'What a lot of letters you do have, dear,' Kate said, 'but I never see you sitting down to answer them as Rose does when her friends write to her.'

'I'm a shocking correspondent,' replied Pearl lightly.

Later that day she told Kate she was going into North-pond to shop, and the older woman was relieved when she had the house to herself. Then the atmosphere seemed to clear. But it was absurd to give way to fancies, and when neither Rose nor Pearl were near her, Kate could persuade herself her fears were nothing more.

✳ CHAPTER 11 ✳

In a small café in Northpond, David and Pearl sat facing each other at a table in a corner.

'If we had to meet,' said Pearl, 'it would have been better to choose a large, popular restaurant, where nobody would be particularly surprised to see us together. It would seem natural then, as though we had met by accident.'

'You don't know Northpond,' answered David. 'If we were seen together at the Metropole, for instance, it would be all over the place within twenty-four hours; a topic to discuss.'

'But there would have been nothing *to* discuss. It might

easily have occurred through chance.'

'Yes – but how uninteresting to believe it. Gossip, you know, has to be lively, and at least slightly scandalous. Nobody is likely to see us here together. This place does very badly and is closing down. Not without reason, for both food and service are poor. I'm sorry about that, Pearl. I'm afraid you won't enjoy your lunch.'

'Oh, what does it matter! I'm not hungry. David, I told you I wouldn't meet you. That day – it was for the first and last time.'

'In your way you're as hard and stubborn as Rose,' he lamented. 'I haven't had a word alone with you, and I had to. You don't realize how wretched I've been. I'm actually putting in more work than necessary at the factory, because it helps me not to think, which shows the state I'm in, as I loathe the place.'

Although he spoke with grievance, there was happiness in his eyes. For him it was joy only to be with her, whatever the circumstances, and Pearl, though she endeavoured to suppress it, felt much the same.

The waitress brought them watery soup and they made an attempt to swallow it, as they might have swallowed medicine.

'We can't go on like this,' said David.

'We're not going on, we're finished,' said Pearl, but she was unable to look at him. 'I told you so. We had a quarter of an hour or less. We stole it, and we shall always remember it, but that was the end.'

He said desperately : 'But how can you want me to marry a girl I no longer love?'

'You are mistaken about that, I think. You do still love her – just as much as you always did. All that happened was that for a short time you caught a glimpse of a different kind of love. You may find that glimpse again, you may sacrifice Rose for it, but it will be for another woman, years hence, possibly, who won't be me.'

'Which means I shall be so bored and disappointed that I shall be faithless to Rose anyway.'

'It means nothing of the sort. Few men, I imagine, are entirely faithful to their wives, but it will depend on Rose how serious an affair it is. She may make you a very satisfactory wife; that is if you are strong now. She has no right to ruin your life, but neither have you the right to ruin hers.'

The waitress changed their plates, and supplied them with fillets of fish and soggy mounds of mashed potatoes. David waited until she left them and then said in an exasperated voice : 'How can you be so objective? It's inhuman. I love you and I want you.'

'I'm sorry.' Pearl shook her head.

'Do you mean you don't care?'

'Of course I care; of course I suffer, but I'm accustomed to suffering. I can bear it. We shall none of us be completely happy for a time, but we shall have our compensations. I shall see you succeed. Rose will be your wife. You will have your play.'

'Oh, I understand how you have planned it,' said David. 'I'm not to give in to her over this matter of my career, but I'm not to make her unhappy in any other way. What if she refuses to give in to me?'

'She won't. You are stronger, because you don't need her as she needs you.'

'Oh darling,' David half whispered, 'when you agreed to meet me here, I thought it meant that you felt as I did, that life was impossible without each other.'

'It isn't impossible, only difficult.'

David looked at her calm and lovely face and was bewildered. A week ago he had held her in his arms and she had responded to him as Rose had never responded. He would never forget it; that sense of time standing still; that certainty of fulfilment and the rightness of life. She also must have known when in his arms that it was her place, that nothing else would do. It was a crime for her to deny it, to insist that the misery of denial could be and must be borne.

But even if he could expound all this, with the eloquence of each right word, it would avail him nothing. She was inflexible.

CHAPTER 12

'But I can't put up with it any longer,' said Kate. 'As I told Rose this morning, if there's one thing I hate it's under-currents.'

Miles realized that Kate's voice had been sounding in his ears for quite a while, though he had given her little attention. It happened so often. She prattled, just as Rose prattled, and one gave her a divided attention, threw in a word now and again. But this was different. There was urgency in her voice; it demanded attention.

'I tried not to tell you, to keep it to myself,' she said.

'To keep what to yourself?' Miles put down his book.

'My worry about Rose, because I'm sure she's unhappy. She denies it though; she said it was all my fancy. Oh Miles, I feel it so badly. She has always confided in me.'

'She's a woman now. You can't expect her to tell you everything.'

'I suppose not.' Kate returned to her knitting, but only for a few minutes, then she burst out afresh. 'She's in her room now; she's been there nearly all day. I asked her if she didn't feel well, but she insisted she was all right, only wanted to be left alone.'

'That may be the best thing for her,' said Miles. 'She seemed ordinary enough at dinner time.'

'But it's Saturday and David hasn't been near all day.'

'Rose was out with him last evening, wasn't she?'

'Yes, but when she came home, I knew she had been crying. I believe she's often in tears just lately. She's taken care I shouldn't get a good look at her, after being out with David; has run off to bed without coming in here to say good night.'

'All lovers have tiffs,' said Miles easily. 'There's nothing you can do. I wouldn't worry too much about it.'

Not for the first time Kate was so exasperated that she could not suppress it. Men were selfish in their refusal to face facts. She said sharply: 'No, I don't suppose you would.

You generally leave all the worrying to me. You won't even admit there's anything *to* worry about, unless it's forced on you.'

'I don't see the good of it that's all.'

Kate sighed heavily by way of reply. After a moment she said : 'You would think Pearl could do something about it.'

At this Miles closed his book with a snap. 'Why Pearl?' he demanded.

'She and Rose are such friends, but she's gone off by herself this afternoon, and Rose is alone too. Of course I know Pearl enjoys her own company, but Rose never did. Pearl must see, just as I see, that Rose isn't herself, and she could have asked her to go with her. But there it is – she's taken out a boat, and she'll be drifting about far from other people.'

'No need to start worrying about Pearl now,' said Miles. 'It's very warm and the sea is calm.'

'I don't worry about her. I always feel she can look after herself. Rose is different. It isn't that she's just younger, there's something helpless about her, something that's easily hurt, and then she doesn't know what to do about it. Miles, you wouldn't think of speaking to David?'

'What about?'

'You could find out what's gone wrong between them.'

'It's not my affair. It will probably right itself.'

Kate had no such hope. She had little to go on, but her instinct warned her that something was profoundly wrong, and that Rose needed the assistance from her parents which she would not voluntarily seek. She said : 'How is David doing at the factory?'

'Just as usual.'

'Working well?'

'I've not heard anything to the contrary.'

'I wish one could feel sure his heart was in it.'

'He'll settle down,' said Miles. 'You'll see – it will be different when he and Rose are married. As it is, he hasn't much of a home life. That's probably responsible for half the trouble.'

'You always think everything is going to be all right, until you find it isn't,' Kate complained.

'What's the good of crossing a bridge until you come to it?'

'How you comfort yourself with those old proverbs, which don't mean half as much as they seem to mean.'

Kate snapped the words at him, and Miles looked at her with surprise. She was usually so even-tempered that such a display of irritation made him realize that she was seriously worried, not merely making what Rose called a fuss. But before he could reply Rose herself came in, and her first words relieved the tension for Kate.

'I'm meeting David at the red rocks,' she said, 'and we shall probably go for a swim. I know you don't approve of mixed bathing, but I can't see any harm in it. My costume has a lot of skirt to it.'

Kate smiled. Not a doubt about that, as she had helped Rose choose the costume. She said cordially: 'Bring David back to tea, why don't you? There's an ox-tongue and salad.'

'Lovely,' said Rose, 'but we may have a meal out. Don't expect me until you see me.'

Miles, mindful of Kate's anxiety, glanced at Rose with more than his usual attention. He could not see that she looked in any way different. She was a nice-looking girl, thought Miles with satisfaction, smart in her gaily patterned cotton dress, over which she was wearing a short white coat. Swimming kit was carried in a small case.

'You look a bit dreary, Mummy,' said Rose, 'why don't you and Daddy go to the first house at the Cosmic. You always find something to amuse you in those music-hall turns.'

She put her arm around her mother's shoulders, and for an instant leant against her. She thought remorsefully that being unhappy made you selfish. You knew you were causing anxiety to the one who loved you better than anything else in the world, and you ignored it, because your heart was full of a pain and anger which could not be communicated. You felt also that your wretchedness was so great, nobody else's could be compared to it.

'There's such crowded houses on a Saturday, and your Dad hates that,' said Kate regretfully, for she would have been glad of the diversion.

'You could go with Pearl,' Rose suggested.

'She's taken out a boat and will probably stay out until

91

after sunset. If you are going to the red rocks you may see her. That's the cove she likes best.'

'Perhaps I shall.'

Rose was no longer angry with Pearl, and would have welcomed a quiet talk with her, but these days Pearl seemed to avoid her. Rose thought she understood. Pearl had withdrawn from the conflict and did not wish to be further involved in it. Quite wise of her, as Rose admitted, for there was no good advice which Pearl could offer her. She would either refuse to say a word or she would side with David, and then they would both say bitter things.

Rose was stubbornly resolved not to give in to David, and he was equally stubborn. He now scarcely seemed to care that he was making her desperately miserable. Last night when she had cried so bitterly, he had made no attempt to comfort her. He had been silent when she reproached him; only when she said she could endure no more of these bitter scenes, he had replied that he couldn't endure them either, that she was poisoning their happiness; that even if he did make a success with his play it would scarcely be worthwhile.

Well, that was satisfactory, wasn't it? It was how she wanted him to feel, and yet she was frightened. You could kill love, and life would be worth little to her if David no longer loved her. Her expression was suddenly so sombre, that Kate said: 'You're all right, aren't you, dear? You haven't seemed yourself today.'

'I'm rather tired, that's all. You worry too much about me, Mummy.'

Rose stroked Kate's neck. It was an old, childish gesture of love, and Kate's heart was full. She looked up at Rose with loving eyes and said: 'I was afraid you and David might have had words.'

'Whatever put that into your head?'

'Just because you looked so white and didn't seem happy.'

'But Mummy, we all have our off-days. There's nothing the matter. Oh dear, it must be terrible to have children.'

'What makes you say that?' asked Miles.

'You do so much for them when they are young, and they depend on you, and then when they're grown up you can't do a thing for them, except worry about them.'

'You've not been much worry to us, my dear,' Miles said.

'You've been a good girl from first to last.'

Kate took the hand which rested on her shoulder and held it against her cheek. She said with love : 'You have been our greatest joy, and when you leave us to get married we shall have nothing but happy memories.'

'I'm glad you can say that,' Rose murmured, half ashamed of the emotional tears which rushed to her eyes. 'I don't know why, but I feel especially glad just this moment, that you can say it.'

A curious sense of poignancy struck her. Suddenly she was acutely conscious of her parents as people, people who would be willing to make any sacrifice for her. All her life, she thought, the giving had been on their side, and the taking on hers. It had seemed natural and right that it should be so, and perhaps she had never been consciously grateful. Even now it was not exactly gratitude that she felt; it was more a heightened sense of awareness. She wanted to say something to them both which they would remember, which might have a tremendous significance in years to come, but she could think of nothing.

They were pathetic to her at this minute – lonely – people growing old with few interests beyond herself. If she were to lay bare her heart to them they would give her advice, and she knew exactly what it would be. They would see everything from her point of view, would hold her blameless, and would support her, and the value to her would be nil.

She bent over Kate to kiss her, and then, more than usually demonstrative, she crossed to Miles and also kissed him. As she stooped to him, the bronze charm on the chain around her neck swung forward, and Miles caught hold of it. 'Do you go into the sea with this round your neck?'

'Yes. Sometimes. The sea water doesn't harm it.'

'Did you ever have the clasp seen to?' asked Kate.

'Not at a shop, but I tinkered with it a bit, and it seems quite safe now.'

Rose moved slowly towards the long windows. She wanted to get away from them and all their unspoken questions, but also wanted to stay with them. But if she did, she would break down, and she couldn't afford to break down. She was overwrought, and she knew it, but just lately she had had terrible feelings; uncontrollable, desperate. She was possessed by a

93

hysterical desire to break up her whole world, and break herself in so doing. It would be worth it, if only for the chance of ending the continuous pain, the sense of being wrong in her very rightness, the conviction that she was driving David away, while longing to hold him; the horror of life and the corroding belief that it was too much for her.

'Go off, and enjoy yourself, dear, don't worry about us,' said Kate.

'Goodbye then,' Rose responded. She lingered for a moment at the door, then forced a smile and went out, leaving the window open. As Miles got up to close it, Kate said : 'What do you make of that?'

'Nothing. What is there to make of it?'

'She seemed odd to me.'

'You're full of fancies these days, Kate.'

'Perhaps I am, but all the time I have the feeling that something is going on we don't know anything about. I wonder if Pearl – she couldn't have anything to do with it?'

'To do with what?' Miles asked impatiently.

'Rose being so changed.'

'I can't see any change in her. It's all in your own mind. She and Pearl get on, don't they?'

'Rose has quite a craze for her – or she did have.'

'Worn a bit thin, has it? Just as well. I've always said it would be a mistake for Pearl to settle here permanently.'

Kate said : 'I've come round to your way of thinking about that. I've nothing against the girl. I'm fond of her, but that silent way of hers makes me uneasy sometimes.'

'You know I never wanted her to come here,' said Miles.

'But that's such a hard thing,' Kate protested. 'Your own daughter. She fairly doted on you, too, when she was a child. Never a week she didn't write to you, though you sent her away. My heart was often sore for her.'

'So was mine,' said Miles heavily. As sore as it was today when he thought of Pearl, which was as seldom as possible. There was nothing he could do now. They were apart, and yet they were close to each other; as close as those in enmity must often be.

Kate said uneasily : 'Miles, there's nothing I ought to know, is there? I've seldom spoken of that poor girl you married before you knew me, but – there was nothing wrong with her, was there?'

'Wrong?'

'Something about her, something she did to turn you against Pearl? She wasn't – unfaithful to you? What I mean is, Pearl *is* your own daughter?'

Miles exploded into anger. 'What a thing to ask me! Her mother was – in that way she was perfection. Poor child – we were married less than a year.'

But had he any right to be angry? He suspected that some such question must have been in Kate's mind for years – and it was his fault. Kate was not clever but she could be shrewd, and the story he had told her had not been a detailed one. He had travelled all over the world for more than a year, and he had met a lovely, high-born Spanish girl who was an orphan, and had married her. Kate had accepted his story, had said little about it during all the years of their marriage. She had said once it was so sad, she preferred to forget it. The poor young thing, leaving her country and her people for his sake, only to die in a strange land. Her attitude had made everything easier for him, and he had been grateful.

How would she have reacted had she known the truth? Knowing her as well as he now knew her, he did not suppose it would have made much difference. A daughter who was half Indian, would have seemed scarcely more foreign than a girl who was half Spanish. He had been a fool ever to deceive her, for that was partly responsible for Pearl's scornful bitterness. But it was too late now to make any confession.

'I'm sorry, dear,' said Kate humbly. 'I don't know what came over me. It was a silly thing, too – for there's the likeness Pearl has to you. Everyone notices it.'

'It shows what a bad father I've been to her, that such a thought crossed your mind.'

Kate shook her head. 'Oh, no, you haven't, dear – not to say bad. I dare say many men feel the same about a child which cost the mother her life. A sort of resentment.'

That was such a shallow but reasonable interpretation of his attitude to Pearl that he seized upon it. 'It's illogical and unjust, but there's something in what you say,' he conceded.

Kate regarded him with wistful affection. She was fully

occupied and unimaginative; not the type to brood. To her the trivialities were important, and she often said she had scarcely a moment to herself; but that was said with satisfaction; she was far from desiring such a moment. Now and again, however, she had been conscious of a barrier between herself and Miles, in the same way that she was now conscious of one between herself and Rose. That made her so uneasy that she refused to consider it for any length of time. Today, though, she was in need of reassurance.

'But I made up to you, didn't I?' she said. 'I know that poor girl was your first love, but you turned to me afterwards; and then when Rose came along . . .'

She broke off, for there was a quiver in her voice. The next thing would be that she came over tearful, and Miles did so hate anything of that sort. But to her surprised gratitude, his voice was kind and gentle as he said: 'I never cared for anyone as I care for you, Kate. And we've been happy.'

'Indeed we have,' she agreed. 'Nobody could have a better husband.'

There was a blur before her eyes, and furtively, she took her handkerchief from her pocket and dabbed at them. Miles was right, there couldn't be much wrong between David and Rose since Rose had gone off to meet him and had said she wouldn't be home for hours. Perhaps she was a bit run-down, getting all upset like this. It mightn't be a bad idea to see the doctor and ask him to give her a tonic.

❋ CHAPTER 13 ❋

Pearl lay stretched out on the sands. She lay on her front, with her arms folded and her face resting on them. She was wearing her swim suit, and the sun poured down upon her bare shoulders; but she could never have enough of the sun, and the dark skin which looked as though it was permanently and becomingly tanned would be no darker after hours of such exposure.

She had been angry, but now she was calm. She knew when

she had lost, and she could accept it. In the future David would go his own way and she would cut her losses; she would be indifferent. Of Brightwell she had had more than enough, and more than enough also of Kate and Rose. In a few days she would announce casually that she was going back to London to live, and not Kate nor Rose nor Miles would be really sorry.

A cat amongst the pigeons, that was what she had been, Pearl thought with a shaken laugh, but the pigeons had escaped unscathed.

David, taking the chance of seeing her when Rose and Kate were out, had briefly told her that he was giving way. The play no longer mattered to him. Graham Bernard could produce it, or he could throw it aside. There had been too much misery over the whole thing. Rose was so wretched that he could not bear it, could not bear to realize he was responsible. Even if she did give way to him, it would mean that she was torn in bits over it, that she would never be happy as his wife.

'And what about you?' Pearl had asked, and he had laughed with bitterness.

There wasn't so much in it for him, whichever way you looked at it. The next few months would be intolerable anyway, even if his play did make a success. Pearl might possess unlimited fortitude, but he did not. In any case his personal life was wrecked, and since Pearl would have none of him, Rose at least might as well be happy.

He was sure now that she never would be happy away from Brightwell, parted from her people, knowing that she had so grieved and disappointed them. But if they could get back to the old footing his conscience would be clear so far as she was concerned.

A prolonged argument was impossible, and Pearl had said coolly that perhaps he was right, and that it was his own affair. She had walked out of the room while he was still trying to explain himself to her.

As though she needed any explanation, as though she did not completely understand that Rose in her weakness had won against her own clear-sighted strength.

It was long since such impotent pain and anger had taken possession of her. Her one craving had been to get away from the place. When Kate had returned, she had told her that the day being so warm she would go sailing. She would probably be out for hours.

Kate made no comment. The warm affection which she had given Pearl had cooled of late, and Pearl did not much wonder at that. Kate no doubt blamed her for having encouraged David in his writing at the beginning, and probably thought that much of Rose's unhappiness was due to her.

And so it was, but only because Rose was Rose; because she was obstinate and narrow and selfish.

Silently, broodingly, Pearl assessed herself. Had she been really base she would have seized the opportunity to destroy Rose. She would not have hesitated over that, had she fulfilled Miles's conception of her; but Miles was stupid, so stupid. He condemned without in the least understanding.

She had never had any intention of hurting Rose; all Pearl had wanted was to help David, and then she would have stood aside. She would have been scrupulous not to interfere with his life or Rose's. Was that base? Probably, and if it would have made her the more harmless, she would have turned to Graham Bernard, giving him little enough, but not deceiving him, knowing that he accepted her as she was, and still considered her well worth having.

It was only Rose who refused to make the smallest sacrifice or concession; Rose who was such an ordinary girl, but whose set plan meant more to her than David's talent, ambition or happiness. Sure that she was in the right, she had broken him down with her tears and reproaches.

Pearl despised herself because she was so much in love with David, selflessly in love, for she cared nothing about herself, as long as the pattern was right for him. Now it never would be. He would commit himself to Rose's planning, and gradually his talent would be smothered; it would die; but not without pain. There might be much sorrow and tension first, while he endeavoured to content himself with a commonplace security.

For Pearl there was not even that. When Kate had persuaded her to stay at Brightwell after Cynthia's death, she had

98

been far from visualizing the secret battle with Miles; guerrilla warfare only vaguely suspected by Kate and Rose. How was it that when she and her father were together, they were both at their worst? Distrust and unwilling love on his side; contempt and unwilling love on hers.

It was strange to look back and to remember that in the beginning there had been nothing bitter in her love, only a child's adoration of a handsome, charming father of whom she saw too little. But that child was a Eurasian. That, of course made all the difference to Miles, with his certainty that nothing good could come from one of mixed blood.

A hand fell on Pearl's bare shoulder, and abruptly she sat upright. She had heard no footstep on the soft sand, but Rose stood beside her.

'Mummy thought you might be here,' said Rose, and squatted down on the sand nearby.

'I moored the boat, but I'm taking it out again,' said Pearl, glancing at her sister who still looked woebegone.

Rose looked round her, and hot as it was she shivered slightly. They could have been alone in an empty world, for there was not a soul in sight, and the lumpy pillars of red rock which gave the cove its name, which usually fascinated them both, seemed ugly and sinister.

'Few people come here,' said Rose. 'There's nothing to come for, not even an ice-cream kiosk. But perhaps that's why you like it. You're happy when you are alone.'

'Sometimes.'

'I hate it. I want to have people around, though just now I don't know how to bear being with Mummy and Dad. I'm always in dread that she is going to break out with a lot of questions. I told her I was meeting David here.'

'Then I expect he'll be along any time.'

Pearl got up and pulled on her towelling wrapper. She walked towards the stone quay and started to unknot the rope which tied her boat to a ring there.

'Please stay, or let me come with you,' Rose pleaded.

'I'd rather be by myself.'

'You're so unkind. Need you be, when I'm feeling so badly about things?'

She spoke in a moaning tone which was unlike her, and

99

which exasperated Pearl. She said : 'You could put everything right in half an hour or less, if you really cared about
David's future.'

'He doesn't care about mine,' Rose complained.

Pearl, who had started to push the boat out to sea, stopped
short and looked at her sister searchingly. What a miserable
little face! Evidently she had as yet no idea that David
intended to give in to her; that she had won. Well then, let
her be unhappy for as long as possible, Pearl thought. Pearl
would not be the one to put her out of her misery.

'You will have to settle your differences for yourself,' she
said stonily.

She would not ask Rose to help her to push out the boat,
and Rose watched her drearily, sitting there on the sands with
her arms clasped round her hunched knees. But the sea was
deep enough, and soon Pearl was able to wield the oars.
With long, sure strokes she rowed away.

Out on the open sea she sighed with content. Now she was
beyond Rose's pursuit, and she could bear what she had to
bear. She drifted along peacefully, half dreaming, with her
eyes half closed. In that waking dream she was happy. David
and she were together, and Rose dispensed with. How long it
lasted she could not have said, but suddenly she was fully
awake, aroused by a sense of shock, a sense of peril.

With dilated eyes she gazed around her. The blue sea was
as calm as a lake; there was not another boat in sight. She
was now a long way from the shore, but she could still see the
gaunt red rocks, and for a moment she fancied that she could
also see a head in a bright yellow bathing-cap; worn by
one who though far away was swimming in her direction.

But that was absurd, Pearl told herself. Her eyesight,
though good, was not as good as that. Even if Rose should
be swimming near the rocks, she would be too far away to
be seen. None the less it was as though she had received
an urgent summons. Something was telling her to row back
to the shore. But she wouldn't, she couldn't! She had escaped
from Rose who must be happy enough now, for David
would have joined her, and would have told her she had
nothing to fear. Still straining her eyes towards the land,
with the oars idle in her hands, Pearl waited in irresolution.

✳ CHAPTER 14 ✳

Kate was playing Patience. It was eight o'clock now, and the girls, she thought, should be in before long. Pearl, at least, would not stay out late, though David and Rose might not put in an appearance until ten or afterwards.

Miles had gone for an evening stroll, as he often did. Sometimes Kate went with him, but she was tired this evening. The heat tried her, and there was scarcely a breeze, though the sun had died down.

The cards were spread out on the centre table, and Kate held a few fan-wise in her right hand. She murmured : 'The nine of hearts goes on the eight of hearts, and then . . . oh dear, there's something wrong. Patience was the right name to give this game. I don't know why I bother.'

She paused to consider the cards and frowned with annoyance, and then a smile broke over her face. Perhaps she could cheat a little. Why not? With a sly expression she manipulated the cards to suit herself, and then aware of her absurdity, she laughed. That had done it, she thought.

She looked up as she heard the outer door open, and exclaimed with surprise as Miles came in, not alone, but followed by David. Immediately, and as usual, her thoughts centred on the larder. She planned a snack meal for the family; sandwiches and cakes and coffee if David intended to stay; though there was only potted meat to use as a filling.

'Oh, here you are,' she said. 'Nice to see you, David. Where is Rose?'

The two men exchanged a glance. They had known this would be Kate's first enquiry. Miles sat down at the table near her, but David stood, a perplexed and anxious expression on his face.

'We wondered if she had come home yet?' said Miles.

Kate stared at him. 'Come home? Rose! But why should she? David would have brought her.'

'Now I don't want to alarm you, my dear, but we hoped

she would be here,' said Miles.

Instantly Kate was terrified: 'What has happened?' she asked.

'Nothing, so far as we know.'

'Then why did you say you didn't want to alarm me? Where *is* Rose? What have you done with her? She's ill.'

Miles said: 'Calm yourself! I went out for a stroll as you know, and coming back I ran into David. He was on his way here, wanting to see Rose.'

'Oh, for mercy's sake, have you upset her again, David?' Kate cried. 'She's been with you the best part of the day. Did she leave you to come home on her own, or what?'

'She didn't leave me. She hasn't been with me.' David looked perplexed and worried.

'But that's nonsense. She said she was meeting you.'

'I don't understand that.'

'David,' Miles put in, 'says that he and Rose had made no arrangement to meet today.'

Helplessly Kate looked from one to the other. She repeated: 'But Rose said . . .'

'Don't get upset, Mrs Shandon,' David soothed. 'I'm sure there's no need. She must be with one of the neighbours.'

'She was to meet you at the red rocks,' Kate said obstinately. 'She went off to meet you.'

'We hadn't fixed anything. The fact is we had an – er – quarrel last evening. A stupid business – nothing really, but I went off without saying I would meet her today. I was at home until half an hour ago. I've been there all day, and then I thought I'd come along to see her, to try to clear things up.'

'I knew there was something wrong,' Kate cried. 'I knew she was half out of her mind with misery, poor child, but when I taxed her she wouldn't own it.'

'It was nothing serious,' David insisted.

Kate glanced at the clock: 'Where can she have got to? It's getting on for nine.'

'Is Pearl in?' Miles asked, and when Kate said that she was not, his expression cleared. 'Then depend upon it,' he said, 'they're together somewhere.'

'Yes, they might be,' Kate agreed, 'but why did she say she was meeting David?'

'Perhaps to avoid being questioned,' said David.

'She often goes off swimming on her own, and you told her it was likely she would find Pearl at the red rocks cove.'

'But where could they be at this hour? I feel something terrible has happened. I've been uneasy all day. I told you there was a change in Rose, that she wasn't like herself, but you said you couldn't see it.'

'I still say it.' Miles put his arm around Kate's shoulders. 'Come now, you mustn't go to pieces like this, and for no real reason.'

Kate shook him off and approached David. She said: 'What did you quarrel about?'

'Nothing important – I've said so.'

'But at one time you and Rose never had a wrong word. What did you do to make her unhappy?'

'Nothing.'

'There must have been something.'

'All the hard words were on her side. She's had her own way from beginning to end.'

'But your way was her way.' Kate was honestly puzzled.

'Was it?'

'Oh, what's come over you, David? What has happened?'

Miles, who had been closely watching David, supported her. 'Yes, you had better explain.'

David flashed back with indignation: 'It's a bit much to be attacked like this because Rose and I had a disagreement which, when I came round here this evening, I had every intention of putting right.'

'But what was there that needed to be put right?' Kate questioned. 'Rose adores you. There's nobody in the world for her but you.'

'Yes, I know. That's why . . . I mean it's because she does think such a lot of me, and I of her, that I've made up my mind to sacrifice everything for her. I told Pearl so . . .'

'Pearl? How does she come into this?' Miles demanded.

David, regretting his slip, said quickly: 'She doesn't come into it, except that she was present one day when Rose and I had an argument, and she thought – well, she thought that I should stand by what I considered right.'

'Go on,' said Miles harshly.

David supposed that now the entire story would come out. Rose, he knew, had kept it to herself, because the thought of all the questioning, and the domestic storm which would follow, was beyond endurance. He said stiffly and reluctantly: 'I sent my play to London, and I had an offer for it – the promise of a production. I wanted to chuck the factory. I wanted Rose to marry me and come to London with me. I hate the grind and the monotony of a business life. I don't care a hang about security. It seemed to me that if Rose really cared she would understand how I felt and take the risk.'

Kate was staring at him with incredulous indignation: 'Throw over all her plans and dreams,' she cried. 'Agree that it was right for you to disappoint your Dad and hers. Let us all down. Behave as though the family business counted for nothing, and all because you've written a play which won a prize of a hundred pounds; though why the Arts Theatre people chose it, is a puzzle to me.'

At first David had accepted patronizing and disparaging remarks about his play with indifference. Having little belief in himself he had imagined they might be justified, but Pearl's confidence in him and her praise, and Graham Bernard's encouragement, though this was on the cautious side, had had their effect. Even in the days when he had thought least of himself, Kate's opinion would have been of no importance to him. She was a nice woman and Rose's devoted mother, but her estimation of any work of art would never have been asked, nor would she have considered herself competent to give one. It was only because he was engaged to marry her daughter that she could see him in no other light. That was maddening, but at a less crucial moment he could have laughed it off. Now, however, it was with resentment that he said: 'It's not only the Arts Theatre. When a first-class manager, a famous man such as Graham Bernard thinks well of a play, then it means something.'

'Graham Bernard!' exclaimed Kate. 'That's the name of Pearl's London friend who called here last week.'

'It was partly because I sent him my play, and he thought it good, that he did call here.'

There was a pause. Kate looked at Miles with consternation, and Miles looked at David with heavy disapproval. He said : 'You gave me your word to drop the play-writing business for the time being.'

'I meant to, but I couldn't.'

Pearl had a hand in that, thought Miles. He admitted that David was a clever chap; he assessed his talent more accurately than either Kate or Rose; though it was not the type of talent he valued; but he was sure David would never have had the resolution to persist in his own way without strong encouragement. He said : 'No doubt Pearl told you, you would be a fool to pay any attention to me.'

'It was entirely my idea,' David maintained.

·'Well, that may be true, or it may be a lie, but at any rate you have played a deceitful game.'

Not for the first time, David considered that point of view and found it amazing. Throughout the last week he had tried to put himself in Rose's position, and had at last concluded that he must seem selfish and stubborn to her as she seemed to him. In the end his pity and remorse had conquered. Pity because he knew he could never give her what she gave him, remorse because he was in spirit unfaithful to her, but Miles with his dictator attitude was a different matter. Detesting conflict, David yet saw that it was likely to persist as long as Miles lived. Married to Rose, he would be living close by and under her father's eyes, and that being so, it was unlikely Rose would ever break away from his influence. A bleak prospect, but now his entire future was bleak, and he would have to accept it. It was more with weariness than defiance that he said : 'I've my own life to consider. I thought when I put it to Rose she would stand by me, but she took a different view.'

'How could you expect her to do anything else?' asked Kate, and looked at him as though he had suddenly become a stranger to her. 'What girl brought up with so much love could bear to break her parents' hearts by going against all their wishes?'

David shrugged : 'It's been known to happen. We even have Biblical authority for it. "Thy people shall be my people, and thy country my country." According to your own creed, Mrs Shandon, a wife is supposed to be subject to her husband.'

Kate retorted superbly : 'Don't be silly. We all take that

with a grain of salt. Besides, you're not yet Rose's husband. She has as much right as you have to think of the future, and to refuse to be dragged down to poverty. Why, your play might be a failure, and not run a week.'

'There's always that chance, but I should have gone on writing, got free-lance work, struggled along.'

'You'd have written to your father, asking for help,' Miles said.

'Yes, that's what you would have been forced to do,' Kate agreed. 'You would never have made out on your own as Rose knew. Poor child, no wonder she has been miserable.'

'I couldn't bear her to be miserable,' said David. 'I've been wretched myself this last week; but as I've told you, I've decided to do what she wants. Bernard can produce the play, but it won't make any difference. I shan't leave here. I shall stay on at the factory, and do my best there, and try my utmost to make Rose happy. It will be years before I think of writing another play.'

'Well, that's something,' said Miles. 'I'm glad you've come to your senses.'

'And not before time,' Kate retorted. 'I'd be better satisfied if you wrote to Mr Bernard and told him you had changed your mind and didn't want the play to be produced.'

David looked at her with a dislike he had the sense to realize was no more than a passing emotion. Though he could think of various uncomplimentary adjectives to apply to Kate, he would in time remember her advice with acrid amusement. He said : 'That would be asking a bit too much. I'm bound to say you seem quite callous over my sacrifice, though you are indignant at the thought of Rose giving up a single thing upon which she has set her heart.'

'It's Rose who belongs to us.'

There was a simplicity in this to soften the heart. So, he supposed, might his own mother have spoken, had she lived. This after all was the crux of the matter, and he could have pitied all parents as Rose had pitied them earlier in the day, because it was a rare thing for them to outgrow their children, though their children might outgrow them.

'I understand that. I know it's tough on you,' he said.

'We don't want to be unfair to you,' said Miles. 'But what *are* you sacrificing? You have had a bit of success and flattery and it has turned your head, and we are trying to prevent you throwing up the most important thing in the world — security.'

'There's no such thing; it's a myth. I might be run over crossing the road; the factory might be burnt to the ground tomorrow.'

Miles instantly demolished what he considered an absurd remark by reminding David that they were well covered by insurance, and Kate chimed in to say that insurance companies were rarely known to go bankrupt, and that such a thing would certainly not happen to the world famous one with which they were concerned.

David, who was now bored with the entire argument, which was useless in any case as he had given way, only wished that Rose would walk in and put an end to it. He could make his peace with her, and once she knew she was to have her own way, she would put everything right. She had her own code and she would be loyal to him then, passionately loyal; nobody would be allowed to say a word in criticism of him, and she would do her best, poor little thing, to make up to him. Nothing would make her believe that his hatred of the factory and his longing for an altogether different life were more than whims he would outgrow. She would throw all her energy into making an attractive home for him, and in every small way she would defer to his opinion. It would be : 'My husband says,' or 'David thinks . . .'

Once married to him, she would be horrified lest people supposed that she was taking the lead. A henpecked husband was a reproach to a really womanly girl, and her self-deception would be sincere and complete. In time, David supposed, it would also deceive him.

But there was no sign of Rose, and Miles, going across to the window and drawing aside the curtain, remarked that it was now very dark.

Kate's maternal anxiety again flared up. 'Oh, where can Rose have got to?' she cried. 'It isn't like her to do such a thing as this. Somehow or other she would have got a message to us.'

'Why should she?' Miles reasoned. 'She doesn't know David

is here. She told us she might be going out for the evening with him, might be late home.'

'What made her say such a thing?' Kate wondered.

'Can't you guess?' said David. 'She knew you had your eye on her, were noticing her, suspecting something had gone wrong. It must have made everything worse for her. She wanted to get away by herself.'

Miles agreed that that was probable, but Kate was indignant. She was Rose's mother, she protested, and she understood her. Rose needed her sympathy, but she was too loyal to David to demand it, knowing what her parents would think of his backsliding. It had been a difficult position for her, poor girl. She loved David, and however badly he was behaving, it would hurt her to have him criticized.

Miles endeavoured to soothe her by saying that she might have cause to worry if Pearl was in, but why should she stay out by herself? He was convinced that the two girls were together.

'Oh, I hope they are, I hope they are . . .' Kate murmured distractedly, starting to pace up and down the room.

And it was at that moment that an agitated knocking on the front door was heard, followed by a prolonged peal of the bell.

✳ CHAPTER 15 ✳

No three figures carved in stone could have stood in more motionless silence. Quicker than the breath of wind the contagion of animal fear ran from one to the other, infecting them all. Then with a visible effort Miles said: 'Better see who it is,' and went to the front door.

He left the living-room door open, and Kate moved falteringly towards it, leaning against it, looking out into the hall. A moment later she said: 'It's Mrs Ford.'

Not a word was spoken by Miles as he admitted Mrs Ford and followed her into the living-room, but he realized, as swiftly as Kate and David realized, that this was no ordinary visit, for Mrs Ford was in a state of considerable agitation. White of face and hatless, she clutched her coat around her, and looked from one to the other.

She had come as a messenger to deliver tragic tidings, that was clear to David, and he shared the fear and anguish which swept down upon the others; but yet that writer's mind of his continued to function, to register details which would come back to him minutely years later. Genuinely pitiful the woman certainly was, but she was also conscious of her importance as the bearer of bad news, and that importance was precious to her, had caused her to press ahead of all others, claiming her rights as the nearest neighbour and Kate's personal friend. Yet now that she was here she wavered, wished she had left such a heartbreaking task to another.

All this, with a cynical detachment, David understood, though his heart was beating in hammer strokes and he tasted the salt of fear in his mouth.

'You're wanted, Mr Shandon,' the woman said, 'I – I came on ahead to tell you. It – it may be all a mistake, but I was down at the shore, down at the shore . . .'

Kate had approached and before Miles could speak she had gripped her by the shoulders. 'What is it?' she demanded, her voice strident.

'They think there's been an accident,' Mrs Ford faltered.

'To our Rose?'

Mrs Ford gulped and nodded. She was near to tears. 'They were saying . . . someone found her clothes near the rocks . . . went to the police station with them . . .'

Miles who had listened in stunned silence suddenly came to life. 'You're certain of this?' he asked.

'Yes . . . yes, I tell you I was there. It was such an awful shock to me, but I thought . . . someone has got to break it to you.'

Miles turned away from her. He said : 'I'm going down there. Come, David.'

'Miles!' Kate cried out in a stricken voice.

He looked at her almost absently. Later, there would be pity for her and a grief to share, but now he could think only of Rose. He said : 'Stay where you are. Mrs Ford . . .'

'I'll look after her,' she promised eagerly.

Miles went out quickly, but David in that moment of heightened perception hesitated. Conscious of Kate's terror, he said, 'Mrs Shandon, I . . .'

With the venom of mortal pain she turned upon him, crying violently : 'You . . . you. If there's harm come to her, it will be you . . .'

David, with a hopeless gesture, followed Miles. Mrs Ford, her eyes sharp with a new curiosity, looked after them. There'd been trouble of some kind then, she thought. It might be that this was more than a simple accident. Heaven pity the poor souls if that was so. She forgot herself completely, and her heart was shaken with pure compassion.

'Now, take it quietly, dear,' she pleaded. 'It may be all a mistake. Just a terrible scare and nothing more.'

If her prayer could work a miracle, that was what it would be, for Kate's blank and ashen face was terrible to behold, and when she spoke it was as though she had not heard the would-be consoling words.

'Are they sure the things belonged to Rose?' she asked in a dull voice.

'I'm afraid so . . . the towel was marked with her name, so they said, and there was her handbag.'

'Oh, it can't be true, it can't be true,' cried Kate distractedly, her hand on her heart to still a pain which might have been physical or mental, but which pierced her with agony.

'You must try to be brave,' Mrs Ford entreated, her voice broken. 'Let me make you a cup of tea.'

'Will they – will they . . .?'

'They'll search for her.'

'I'm going down there,' said Kate. 'I can't believe it – but she got cramp last year, when she was in the water. Since then I've always been afraid.'

'They may find her on the sand-dunes, taken ill, fainted,' Mrs Ford comforted. 'They'll bring her home, dear. Don't think of going down there, please don't. It might be such a shock to you.'

'Shock!' Kate looked at the other, and scorned her for a fool. Hadn't she already taken such a shock as she would never forget or get over? Even if Rose walked into the room now, it was something she would recall with shuddering horror for the rest of her life.

'Oh, why did I let her go, why didn't I stop her?' she cried, and as Mrs Ford put her arms round her, she violently cast her off, and ran into the hall.

'You can't go like that . . . your coat,' Mrs Ford cried. 'Oh, here's one hanging up.'

'Leave me alone,' Kate protested, but she was passive as Mrs Ford gently forced her arms into the sleeves of the coat, and she suffered her when she said: 'I'll go with you, dear.'

A weakness, a deadly sense of faintness, was stealing over Kate, but she fought against it. Rose couldn't be dead; it was impossible. It seemed only a few minutes ago that she had smiled at her, had bent to kiss her. Her lovely, loving girl! As she sped down the road, with Mrs Ford clinging to her arm, she turned her eyes away from the sea, for it was unbearable to look at it.

CHAPTER 16

All the lights were on as Pearl opened the front door with her latch-key. Instinct told her that it was empty, but she purposely hushed her footsteps, walking into the living-room almost soundlessly. Her hair was blown with the wind, and she mechanically smoothed it as she looked around her. A wild irrelevance flashed into her mind.

There was a book she had read, or a story, about a ship, a mysterious ship called – what was it called? Oh, yes, the *Marie Celeste.* It was found drifting, and when members of the crew of another ship went aboard, it was deserted, though all looked as though people had been there only a few hours before. There had been a meal set, and a baby's dress half-made, still in the sewing-machine, and a book turned down as though someone had been reading it. But what had become of the crew and the captain's wife was never discovered.

This room gave one the same impression. All the signs of recent occupation, but the sense of death heavy on the air. She saw the scattered playing cards on the table, and the thrust-back chair. The fire still smouldered in the grate, a folded newspaper lay upon the sideboard; but the silence had an unearthly quality.

She herself felt nothing more than a nagging emptiness. She was not hungry, but there was the need to eat. She went into the kitchen and looked around her. She found milk and biscuits in a tin and some cheam cheese.

Standing there, she drank the milk slowly and ate the biscuits spread with cheese finding that she was ravenous, which wasn't surprising, for she had had nothing but a cup of tea since lunch-time.

She could not think at all. She had locked a door on thought, and was still without feeling. It was as though every nerve in her body had died; but she washed-up the glass and the plate she had used, cast a glance around to see that the kitchen was as tidy as usual, and returned to the living-room.

An independent part of her mind, functioning in a clear and rational manner, told her that this curiously detached attitude was a manifestation of shock. She did not want to recover from it. It was a little death, and she could sink in it, far beyond grief or regret.

She made a perfunctory attempt to tidy the room, and then ceased. It wasn't worth worrying about. But presently she put her hand into her coat pocket and brought out a small, bright object. She held it up and looked at it. Rose's bronze disc; her sun-god charm on its thin, gold chain.

A sense of possession was her first awareness. The charm was hers; nobody should take it away from her. She had wanted it, and most things she wanted came her way.

What a careless girl Rose had been. Time and again Kate had complained of her carelessness, and had told her more than once that she ought to take the chain to be mended, because the clasp was insecure. But Rose had never got round to doing it.

Pearl thought how much better care she would take of this ancient treasure. She would not wear it until a new clasp had been fixed to the chain.

The sound of a key turning in the lock of the front door brought her back to reality. Her hand closed on the charm, concealing it, as Miles came into the room. He walked slowly, and with lowered head, and sat down heavily on the settee. Something stirred within Pearl; her feet and hands began to tingle, as though the blood which had been icy and congealed now started to run freely once again.

'I wondered if you would be here,' said Miles, and as Pearl did not answer him he added : 'You know?'

'Everyone knows,' said Pearl, her voice sounding strange to her, as though it did not belong to her. 'People were talking as I walked through the village.'

She shivered, for that had been a horrible moment, overhearing the conversation of scattered groups collected along the road; but it had been dark enough for nobody to notice her as she fled homewards.

'Where were you?' asked Miles.

'Watching the pierrot show on the pier.'

'We hoped she was with you until somebody found her things and then . . .'

'They've found her?'

'Washed up on the rocks.'

The words, uttered with difficulty in a dullness of anguish, were an almost unendurable pain to her. It was as though Pearl tore herself from the last deadening effects of an anaesthetic, and was once more mercilessly alive. She said in a voice that was no more than a whisper : 'Father, I don't know what to say. Was it – how do they think it happened? The sea was calm.'

'Cramp. She'd had it before. They've taken her – they've taken her to the . . . to them . . . there'll have to be an inquest.'

Pearl asked, 'And Kate?'

'They will tide her over the worst. She had a faint turn – heart, the doctor says. She will be all right, but they thought it best to take her to the cottage hospital. They'll give her drugs – she'll sleep.'

Ah, who could bear this, thought Pearl, hearing him groan, seeing him cover his face with his hands. A passion of pity wrenched her. She murmured his name, and moved nearer to him.

'I never thought a man could be so alone,' said Miles.

Pearl knelt by his chair and put her hand on his knee. Few had seen her look as she looked now. Love and a boundless compassion in her eyes. 'You have me,' she said.

Miles put his hand on her hair. It was as though a dim

realization of her unquenchable love reached out to him and comforted him. He said: 'Yes – yes, I know. My poor child.'

'I can be as much to you as she was,' said Pearl. 'I can be more to you than she was.'

She was back in the days of her childhood, when she had known of the existence of Kate and Rose, but had not imagined they could come between Miles and herself. How could she, loving him so dearly, ever be the outsider?

'I thought it was over,' Pearl said, 'but now I know it isn't, that it can never be over. You can't kill the past. I would still put you first – before anyone – as my mother did.'

Fear struck Miles, and doubt narrowed the eyes which searched her face. 'You weren't jealous of Rose? You were fond of her?' he questioned.

'Oh, yes.'

The casual admission strengthened Miles's doubt, forced a new though unformulated fear upon him. He said slowly: 'There was this quarrel with David.'

'Rose would have got her own way with him,' said Pearl. 'He meant to give in to her. He wrote to me saying so. The post came while Rose was still upstairs, getting dressed.'

'Did you tell her?'

'Why no. He said he would be round some time, and I was just going out.'

'Wouldn't it have been natural, sisterly, as you knew she was in distress, to have told her?'

'It didn't occur to me.'

That was the truth. Pearl had been far from considering Rose's feelings. She had been angry with her, and scarcely less angry with David. She had come near to despising him. Had she followed her first impulse she would have packed all her belongings and left Brightwell on the instant, without explanation. Better if she had perhaps, though at the time she had thought of Kate and her adherence to convention. Kate had been good to her and she would have been much distressed by an abrupt departure which would have been difficult to explain to the neighbours whose opinion meant so much to her. Because of that, Pearl had decided to stay for another few days, to explain casually that friends of Cynthia's had asked her to go abroad with them. Thus the decent reticences would have been preserved. There would have been no rancour. Kate would have been regretful. Rose would have concealed her relief, and Miles – well, he also would have been relieved, thankful that the conflict between his love and his fear was over.

'There's something I don't understand here,' said Miles. 'You were in David's confidence; you sympathized with him, helped him. No,' as Pearl looked at him sharply, 'he didn't tell me, but I'm sure. Somehow you came between them.'

Pearl sat back on her heels, looking at him. It flashed upon Miles that so had her mother often sat. It had been her favourite, her natural position; at his feet, looking up at him with her dark eyes soft for him. Strange that he should remember at such a moment; but memory of her was constantly thrusting its way to the surface, though she had been dead so many years.

'David,' said Pearl, 'would have told Rose today that everything was to be as she wanted it to be.' And then as Miles was silent, she added pleadingly : 'Father, why need you go into all this – now? Rose's death had nothing to do with David. She had cramp – poor Rose.'

'Yes – poor Rose.'

Miles got up while Pearl still sat crouched on the floor. Briefly, her love and her caressing touch had been sweet to him, but they were sweet no longer. 'Does it mean anything at all to you?' he asked abruptly.

Her eyes widened, it might have been with fear, it might have been with reproach. She said : 'I'm terribly sorry.'

'Come here. Let me look at you.' His hands fell heavily upon her shoulders as he gazed into her eyes. 'Am I unjust to you?' he asked.

But there had always been injustice, and they both knew it, and for that he probably blamed himself more than Pearl had ever blamed him. She said : 'I've not complained.'

'You are like your mother – so like her. Everything given up; devotion, surrender, trust, and yet . . . something in her which I could never reach, never understand. It kept us apart and it has kept you and me apart.'

So might a man have spoken who was half-dreaming, but

striving to pierce through the shifting mists of unreality. That first love, the months of his brief marriage had had the same quality; sweet and spellbound.

'Don't let it – not any longer,' Pearl pleaded.

She had never loved him better, never had more pity for him or more understanding. Now was the moment when love submerged and denied could be released, obliterating resentment. Forgetful of all else she put her arms around his neck, and as she did so, the charm clasped in her hand fell to the ground. There was a stupefied moment while they both gazed at it, and then Miles turned horrified eyes upon her.

'Rose's !' he gasped.

Pearl, inwardly raging at herself for her carelessness, stooped to recover the charm. She said calmly : 'Yes. I found it.'

'Found it? But Rose was wearing it when she left here. When I last saw her – alive – it was round her neck.'

'I found it,' Pearl repeated.

'You've seen her since we did,' Miles accused. 'You – she and you were together. What's at the bottom of all this? Tell me the truth.'

The moment of peace, of understanding, the chance of a complete mental and spiritual reconciliation had passed. Pearl knew and accepted it with a bitterness of spirit which Miles would never realize, which was beyond his range.

'But I've already told you the truth,' she said hopelessly.

'You've told me lies. Ever since you came here you've been playing your own game – against Kate and Rose. I knew it, if they didn't.'

Mingled with Miles's anguish and horror there was a sense of justification which upheld him. He had been right, he told himself. Though he had fathered Pearl, and in his tormented way loved her, she was in spirit none of his. His instinctive withdrawal from her had been a natural, a healthy reaction.

'What did you do to Rose?' he demanded. 'How did you come by that charm? Give it to me.'

'No.' Pearl stepped back from him.

'Take care I don't do you a mischief,' Miles said thickly.

Pearl gazed at him unflinchingly. She hated him. She could

have wept; she could have prayed to him. She could have explained, but he would not have believed her. She could goad him and see him wince; see him possessed by his demon; be aware of her own power.

'It's mine,' she said, in a voice which was slow and controlled. 'The charm is mine. You heard Rose say so. She said she would leave it to me in her will.'

Miles heard Pearl's voice through a storm which thundered in his ears. His outstretched hands found her throat and fastened upon it, crushing it relentlessly. She fell backwards from him, across the settee, and he saw her face swimmingly beneath his own; saw its startled whiteness, its dilated eyes.

And then, as once before that day, there came a knocking on the door, loud and demanding, and as suddenly as he had seized Pearl, Miles released her, stood back from her. He heard her drawing her breath in difficult gasps, met her eyes which no longer loved or pitied him.

The knocking on the door continued, and Pearl raised herself on her elbow. She fingered her throat as she said: 'You'd better open the door. They seem to be getting excited.'

The tide of murderous rage receded, and Miles was aghast at himself. He had wanted to kill her; not only to hurt and to punish her, but to take her life. He said stammeringly: 'Pearl, I didn't mean . . .'

His voice might be broken and trembling, but hers was cool, as she said with little expression: 'Whoever it is hammering like that, may think you have put an end to yourself through grief.'

That light, unconcerned voice! Miles could only wonder at her, as he turned away to open the door. Pearl quickly straightened her disordered dress, turned up the collar of her coat to hide the throat which Miles's brutal grip might well have marked. She heard Mrs Ford say: 'Oh, Mr Shandon, I got such a fright. I knew you were in, and not being able to make you hear – well, I was afraid, knowing you were alone.'

Pearl moved towards the open door, saying with composure: 'Come in, Mrs Ford. My father wasn't alone, as you can see.'

Admitted, Mrs Ford made a little rush at her, put her arms round her, and was suffered to do so. She had cried steadily for the last hour, and her face was disfigured by her tears : 'Oh, my dear, what a relief,' she babbled. 'Nobody knew where you were. Poor Rose, poor girl, and her mother taken ill and in hospital.'

'Yes, it's terrible,' said Pearl.

'My husband walked home with your father,' Mrs Ford went on, 'but he seemed to want to be alone, and so he left him. But afterwards we talked it over, and we thought it would be better for him and for you, too, not to have to sleep here tonight. We thought that a bit of company would help you over these first bad hours.'

'That was very kind of you,' said Pearl, gently releasing herself from the other's embrace.

'Then will you both come along to us at once, dear? I've got supper ready, and we have two spare bedrooms, as you know. My hubby and your father get on well together. Make him come with you, dear. It will be better for him than to be alone.'

Pearl murmured consentingly, 'Yes, thank you – I'd like to be with you tonight, and it would be better, much better for Father and me.'

❋ CHAPTER 17 ❋

Carrying a rubber hot-water bottle, Mrs Ford came into the spare room where Pearl was to sleep. She tucked it away between the sheets and said : 'That'll be a comfort to you tonight, dear; shock makes you feel chilly, however warm the weather may be. I'm glad Tom persuaded your father to take a tot of whisky. We're teetotallers as a rule, but it's as well, we always say, to keep a bottle in the house in case of illness, or some emergency.'

'How right you are,' Pearl murmured, and wished that Mr Ford had offered her a drink. She would have welcomed it. However, the idea had not occurred to the good man, who imagined that a cup of tea was all a woman could possibly need.

She watched Mrs Ford as she bustled about, taking off the bedspread, plumping up the pillows. The room which had not yet been occupied during the Fords' short sojourn there, for the children were still away at school, was very chill and neat and fresh. Mrs Ford switched on the electric fire, and Pearl stood close to it, glad of its reviving heat. She had taken off her coat on sitting down to supper, which neither she nor Miles could make more than a pretence of eating, but there had been a scarf in one of its pockets, and she had twisted it cravat-wise about her neck.

Possibly this kind, shallow, chattering woman had saved her life. That was a strange thought. If she had guessed it, how thrilled and horrified she would have been.

Pearl was neither horrified nor afraid. Miles would remember that incident far oftener than she would remember it.

'Now you will take two aspirins, won't you, dear?' Mrs Ford said, 'and they will help you to sleep. You have a hard time in front of you; no doubt about that; but you're a brave girl and will get through it.'

'I hope so,' said Pearl with some doubt, and then with an eye to future eventualities, she explained : 'You see I had planned to leave here tomorrow. Some friends of mine in London wanted me to go abroad with them.'

'Oh, but my dear, you can't go now. You surely couldn't wish to go,' Mrs Ford expostulated. 'Poor Mrs Shandon will need you, and besides there is bound to be an inquest. So dreadful for your poor father, but having you here will be a comfort to him.'

'I shall have to send a telegram to my friends and explain,' said Pearl. 'I may join them later. But of course I shall stay as long as I am needed here.'

'Mrs Shandon will have enough to bear without losing you as well,' said Mrs Ford. 'I'm sure the way she spoke of you, you might have been her own daughter.'

Pearl sighed : 'Now that she has lost Rose she will find I am a very poor substitute. Of course I shall do my best, but it may be that after a time she and Father will be happier alone together. I can only wait and see.'

The other agreed : 'It's impossible to make plans now. I'm so dreadfully sorry for you. You do know there's nothing I won't do to help?'

Pearl said gratefully that that was already clear, and then she sat down on the side of the bed looking so inexpressibly weary that Mrs Ford, though she would have been glad to talk longer, was forced to say good night.

When she had gone, Pearl started to undress, and then when she was in her nightgown, she went to the dressing-table mirror and examined her throat. To her relief she saw that there were only faint marks upon it. These would probably develop into bruises, but they would not be very notice-able. They could be concealed under cream and powder.

With her chin in her hands she sat staring at her reflection. The future was one of gloomy uncertainty. It was true, as Mrs Ford had said, that she could not leave for a while though it would be terrible to stay. She would not think of Rose to-night. For Rose all was over, and perhaps she was fortunate. Of Miles she could not think without bitterness and pain but upon David her thoughts might now rest, and gradually a sense of tranquillity came to her.

Out of all the misery, good might result for David. He was no longer fettered, and when he had recovered from his natural sorrow, he would realize it. Hours ago she had been angry with him, but now as she imagined his unhappiness she longed to be with him. Not that she could say a word to con-sole him, but her very presence would be consolation. He would not think of her now as the lover denied to him, but as the one whose existence was solace.

For the future as it concerned herself and David, who could say? It might be that Rose's hold on him in death would be stronger than in life. Her remembered personality, natur-ally glorified, would not be easily forgotten. But whether he treasured his lost love, or whether he set himself to forget it, David would still write. That ingrained ability could only die for him when he also died, and with his writing she could help him, whatever happened.

She got into bed and the pillow was cool to her cheek, though she hugged the hot-water bottle to her, grateful for its warmth. She remembered the aspirin bottle which Mrs Ford had left on the bedside table, and she sat up again to take three tablets instead of the usual two, swallowing them with water poured from the carafe.

Sleep fell upon her in a heavy wave. But not a restful sleep. In her unconsciousness she was plagued by the memory which she would not permit when she was awake. She was out on the sea, half-dreaming, blissfully content, to be aroused and possessed by fear; by dread. The sea was no longer glittering beneath the sun, but dark and still and menacing. It was heavy and dead, and it was an effort for any swimmer to make headway. She saw Rose's pale and exhausted face, and watched the weakening flail of her arms. She was there to help, but she did not help – or could not. Irresolute she sat motionless, with the oars in her hands. She was indifferent – she did not care. A prayer came to her on the wings of the wind, but she closed her ears to it.

She woke with a cry on her lips and bathed in sweat. Her trembling hand went out to switch on the light. It wasn't like that, she thought; it wasn't her fault. She had left Rose on the sands, waiting as she supposed, for David.

But after that – what happened then? prompted a silent accuser.

'Nothing happened,' she retorted aloud.

She was awake now and unafraid; but it occurred to her that she had been warned. Nobody must know that she had been near the spot where Rose had drowned. Miles might suspect incredible things, but he could not verify them.

✸ CHAPTER 18 ✸

Days passed. The funeral and the inquest were over. Kate weak and shattered, left the hospital and came home.

Miles and David and Pearl had all given evidence at the inquest, though they had been unable to tell the Coroner's jury anything of importance. Pearl avowed that she had not seen Rose that day, and David said the same. Miles revealed that Rose had had an attack of cramp the year before when he had been swimming with her, and that she might have perished then, had he not been at hand to bring her to shore. Rose had promised him that in future she would be careful not to get out of her depth, but she must have forgotten that promise. When the Coroner asked if it had been her habit to swim in such a lonely spot, Miles said he knew she was fond of that particular cove, and although, because of its distance from the town, few people did bathe there, it was a cove which was considered especially safe.

The verdict of Death by Misadventure was a foregone conclusion. Guiltily, Miles and David avoided one another's eyes, for neither had told the exact truth. There had been no mention of a quarrel or of Rose's unhappiness. But Pearl, white-faced, held her head high and David did not guess, and Miles could not be certain, she had anything to hide.

David and Pearl had no chance to exchange a word, and thereafter, when Kate came home, Pearl was fully occupied.

Kate was ill and weak and unspeakably wretched, and she clung to Pearl which surprised Miles when he remembered how she had said she would not be sorry if Pearl left them. If her quiet manner had once made Kate uneasy, now she welcomed it. Mrs Ford called frequently, as did other neighbours, but Kate shrank from their well meant sympathy.

She did not want to talk of Rose, though she constantly thought of her, and Pearl endeavoured to build a wall around her. Visitors were tactfully dealt with, and Kate, within her walled enclosure, slowly and painfully recovered her strength; wept undisturbed when it relieved her to weep, and was not required to make the effort which all her acquaintances were so certain it would be beneficial for her to make.

Pearl did the housekeeping, lifting all responsibility from Kate's shoulders. She seemed to know by instinct when Kate required her company, or when she preferred to be alone. She was always at hand when she was wanted.

Kate, thought Miles, appeared to need Pearl more than she needed him. He wondered at it, and whether he was grateful or the reverse, he could not have said. It was impossible to communicate his suspicions to his broken wife, but he brooded over them and avoided Pearl as much as possible. He had never fully understood her, but now she was an enigma to him, and he dared not probe too deeply into his own mind.

Sometimes when he watched her, saw her thoughtfulness for Kate, realizing that she was caring for her as efficiently, as tirelessly as she had cared for his sister, his heart smote him. What sort of a man was he, that he could believe his own daughter capable of such wickedness? But then he would glance at Pearl's closed face with its quiet, folded lips, its deep eyes, and wonder what thoughts lay behind that calm exterior. When he recalled the violence with which he had treated her, he was baffled. He made excuses for himself, but he was ashamed.

He had accused her of having a hand in Rose's death on evidence which was no evidence at all. She was in possession of the charm which Rose had been wearing when she had gone out of her home for the last time; but although it was a strange coincidence, it was by no means impossible that she might have found it. She had wanted the thing, of course, had coveted it, but why should he constantly read into that a sinister meaning? Had not Rose openly coveted many of Pearl's possessions?

His always difficult love now seemed to be smothered beneath layers of conflicting fears. Fear of himself, of her, of the future. He was desperately alone, more alone than Kate, for she had her ill-health to deaden her grief. She did not doubt the justice of the inquest verdict and she believed in Pearl.

She did, however, nourish an implacable wrath against David. She refused to see him, and although Miles said something about being sorry for the chap, Kate would have nothing to do with such weakness. Miles wondered briefly what was happening about David's play, but as he never voluntarily spoke to Pearl, he could not question her.

Others praised Pearl's devotion to Kate, but Miles distrusted that also, and he was relieved when Kate's only sister wrote to suggest coming to them on a short visit, after which she would take Kate away with her to stay with her at her home in Hampshire.

Kate, wrote Emmeline Thorpe, needed a change of scene. It was the one thing which would help her to recover from her bereavement. The doctor, when consulted, agreed with that, and Pearl for the first time in weeks felt able to relax. Kate, though she had not seen much of her sister of late years – though she was attached to her and liked her husband and children – perceptibly brightened after receiving her letter and Pearl thought with relief that she had given all the service required of her and would soon be free.

Her sense of bondage had been so great that the word 'free' had a peculiar sweetness. Every time she and Miles came in contact she was aware of an inward flinching. His silence was unnerving; so was the long, deep, gaze he occasionally subjected her to.

She had been extremely practical, gathering up Rose's belongings and stowing them away in her room which seemed still to belong to her, speaking of Rose occasionally to Kate when her step-mother seemed to want to talk to her, behaving as though she and Miles were on ordinary terms; but the strain had told on her.

Kate, self-absorbed, noticed nothing, but for Pearl the Brightwell bungalow had become a prison. Her self-control was no longer natural, for she knew well what was passing in Miles's mind. The ghost of Rose moved between them, and he must be aware of it, as she was.

Would she break down the barrier if she could? Pearl did not know. She had played a part for so long. It had been forced upon her by pride, by her rejected, outraged love. Miles would never now believe that in many ways she was as ordinary, as normal as Rose had been. She had had a different upbringing, far more experience of the world, and her father had made it plain that to him she was a strange, unpredictable being. But Cynthia had not found her strange, and she had laughed at what she called 'Miles's superstitious phobia'. Pearl was only different from other girls of her age because her father had insisted that she must be. That belief was ingrained in him, and often Pearl believed it. If she was to tell him what really happened on that last day of Rose's life, he would never believe her. But some day – some day, she would have to tell one who could. Would that be Graham Bernard? No fantastic story told by her would be too difficult for him to credit.

One day, shortly before Emmeline Thorpe was due to arrive, Pearl sat on the window-seat in the living-room. She was finishing the cloth she had started to embroider for Kate weeks ago but presently the work dropped from her hands. She stared out at the sea and loathed it, though there were boats upon it now and people were bathing and children building castles on the sands.

Then she heard the gate click and saw a woman walking up the pathway to the bungalow. She stirred herself for Kate, who was drowsing in her bedroom, must not be disturbed. She had had a prolonged fit of crying that morning, and was worn out. Mindful of this, Pearl went quickly to the front door before the visitor had time to knock or to ring the bell.

To her surprise the caller was Mrs Reever, dressed in her best and looking apologetic. She said : 'I hoped I should find you in, Miss. I heard you were looking after Mrs Shandon and were scarcely ever out. I wanted to have a few words with you.'

'Come in, and I'll make some tea,' said Pearl. 'It's nice to see you again.'

She meant it, for Mrs Reever seemed to bring into this grief-haunted place a touch of normality. It occurred to Pearl with surprise that for weeks she had scarcely given a thought to David. She had thought she was in love with him, but that must have been a delusion, for she hadn't missed him or wanted him. Caught up in a world of hallucination he had been completely unreal to her. But now it struck her that in a life of haunted dreams the real people could not approach one, and looking at Mrs Reever she was aware of a quickening vitality, as though the other's sturdy, sensible personality had the power to sweep away the cobwebs which clouded her mind.

Mrs Reever drank her tea and smiled at Pearl and pitied her pale face. She was still a lovely young lady, she thought, but probably far too much had been put upon her.

'Mr Page is away,' she said. 'He had to go to London on business, and Mr David is alone. I know his heart is set on seeing you, but that poor girl's parents have turned against him, he says, and he's not welcome here any longer. You came to see him once, Miss, and I'm taking it upon myself to ask you if you'll do the same again.'

Pearl hesitated. 'I'd be glad to,' she said at last, 'but I can't leave Mrs Shandon in the daytime. For the last few weeks I've been out only to do the shopping, and then I've had to rush through it, for I'm afraid to leave her alone, and she won't let me ask anyone to come in and sit with her, though several have offered.'

'But you can't go on like that. It's not fair to you. Anyone would be sorry for Mrs Shandon but I've been angry too, for the way she's treated Mr David who wasn't to blame for that poor girl's death, and to my thinking put up with a lot from her.'

'You mustn't misjudge Mrs Shandon,' said Pearl. 'She's not herself, and it's all coming to an end for me, for her sister will be here in a few days, and then I shall be going away.'

'I hoped you might be able to come round one evening, Miss. Mr David is at the factory all day. He couldn't give up and he didn't want to. It took his thoughts off the tragedy.'

Pearl weakened : 'I might manage this evening. I do go for a walk sometimes after my father gets home. I would like to see David before I leave, if only to talk about his play. I had a note from Mr Bernard to say he had written to him about it.'

'He had a contract from him,' said Mrs Reever, 'that's what he told me, though I don't know what he did about it.'

'I'll be around at seven or a little later,' Pearl said.

Mrs Reever smiled approval. 'You'll be alone and can talk, and I'll see you have a nice little supper,' she promised.

❋ CHAPTER 19 ❋

The drawing-room at David's home had been little used for years. It was an attractive room which David's mother had furnished to her own taste. After her death it had been too poignant a reminder to Joseph Page. There his wife had entertained her friends, played on the piano, sat knitting socks and pullovers for David, written her letters.

She had not cared for the rather gloomy dining-room, with the result that of late years Joseph Page had entrenched himself there, smoking and reading and paying little attention to his son who more often than not was with Mrs Reever in the kitchen quarters.

But the drawing-room was in use this evening. Hearing that

Pearl would be calling David had made hasty and eager preparations. Dust covers had been removed from the furniture, flowers had been bought, and as the evening was chilly, a fire had been lighted in the grate.

All was cheerful when Pearl was ushered into the room by Mrs Reever, and David sprang up to welcome her. She wore a thin black silk dress and looked beautiful, as he had known she would look, but she was thinner, and her eyes were shadowed. Clasping her hands, he said : 'I was afraid that you mightn't be able to get away. I knew Reevy had it in her to call on you, but I didn't tell her to. I understand how the Shandons feel about me, it's natural, and although I wrote you didn't answer.'

'Everything has been held up in my mind. I can't explain,' said Pearl. 'It was as though there was no future, only the present, which meant looking after Mrs Shandon and thinking of Rose. It's only three weeks since she died. Not long to give to her. I've been living in a dream, David; a horrible dream. I'm glad Mrs Reever called. She woke me up.'

'I've thought of Rose too – incessantly.' David gently urged Pearl into a big chair near the fire, looking at her anxiously, observing the change in her. She had always been slender, but now she was definitely thin; her hands as she held them to the fire had a transparent quality. David was puzzled and distressed, and almost unbearably happy to have her there.

'Was it difficult for you to get away?' he asked.

'Oh no, my father had his tea, and then I said I was going out. I have my key and can let myself in at any time. He won't notice.'

David knelt before her, and put his arms round her; his head rested against her breast and he felt her hand on his hair. He hadn't planned this approach. Pearl had let him drop out of her life, and might never have cared as much as he cared. He could not now think of Rose, only of Pearl, and of the sweet wonder of being together. Love was natural and beautiful, and all the future was suddenly clear to him.

'How soon can you come away with me?' he asked simply, and as simply she answered : 'Next week probably. Kate's sister will be here on Monday, and she will look after her.'

'Thank heaven! I couldn't wait much longer.'

'Nor could I, now that I'm awake.'

He raised his head, cupped her face in his hands and said : 'Did you think you had stopped loving me?'

'I didn't think of you at all. It was like a kind of illness.'

'Shock?'

'I suppose so.'

She was vulnerable; no longer in command of the situation, and David felt older, and endowed with a sense of responsibility. 'Don't go back there again. Come away with me tonight,' he said.

'I can't do that. I must stay with Mrs Shandon until her sister is here to take over, and you and I must make plans. There's so much I have to tell you – about myself.'

'Not a word until you want to tell me, until you *have* to tell me. Then I'll listen.'

'But I can't marry you, David. I can't. There are reasons.'

'All right – you think you can't – and you needn't until you are ready, but you will. Oh, darling, there's nothing for you to worry about, nothing at all. I'll settle everything.'

Pearl said in surprise : 'You must have done a lot of growing-up these last few weeks, and I feel quite weak and helpless, but that won't last. I've been asleep so heavily and so horribly. Don't expect me to make any promises, except that I'll come away with you, give you what I can – but not marriage.'

'I'm not asking for a single promise. Darling, you're ill, and you won't be well until you leave this place. I'll do everything possible to make things easier, but you must let me look after you.'

He kissed her. Her lips beneath his were cold, but she moved closer into his embrace, as though there she might find warmth. She said : 'I want you to look after me.'

But how strange it would be if he could, she thought; if there were indeed hidden reserves in him which she had not suspected, for she had never been looked after. Cynthia had loved her, but even when a child she had treated her as an adult; Miles had always credited her with an uncanny wisdom.

'We must get away without anyone knowing,' she said. 'I've gone through too many scenes.'

'Lord, so have I!' David spoke with fervour. 'We'll certainly make plans, but not tonight. I want you to rest and be happy.'

'I wish I could be sure you love the real me,' she said wistfully. 'You know so little about me. Some people think me – strange.'

'Why do they?'

'Well, I'm only half-English, and I have a violent temper. I can be arrogant and proud and hateful, and perhaps unscrupulous. I think, too, there are times when I'm a little crazy. I haven't been really sane these last weeks. I've seemed quiet and efficient but I felt nothing at all, not even love for you.'

'I doubt if you do love me properly – yet,' said David. 'You've been so harassed. We both have. You were attracted to me, and you thought I could write, but I was a bit spineless, wasn't I? I can see that now. I ought to have cleared out and left Rose to follow me or not as she chose, but I was too fond of her and too sorry for her; and I felt guilty because I knew that loving you, I had so little to give her. But now – we can be happy and know we are not hurting her. What a relief to come out into the open. I shall feel like shouting it in the streets.'

'You won't regret it?'

'Leaving the treadwheel? Not likely.'

'It may not be easy at first. There may be disappointments.'

'What of it? I shall never hear a factory hooter without a shudder of relief.'

'Poor Rose,' said Pearl, realizing that David's memory of her would be always connected with the life he loathed. 'I was fond of her, you know, in my way. I could never have hurt her by taking you away from her. It would have been such a long desolation for her. Death was easier; it must have been all over in a few minutes.'

'Perhaps – one can't be sure.'

But Pearl had already decided this in her mind, for her

129

own consolation. She said : 'She held that childish quarrel against me. She must have done – to accuse me as she did that day.'

'In the heat of the moment. We shall have to forget all that.'

'Are you good at forgetting?'

'I don't know. These last weeks I've not forgotten for an hour. It has been hell. But if one is strong enough, one can put things at the back of one's mind.'

'I suppose that's true,' Pearl agreed.

David got up as Mrs Reever came in with a tray. She said : 'I thought you'd like your supper in here, by the fire. Put up the card table, Mr David, please, and then I can set it all out for you.'

It was the first meal which Pearl had enjoyed for weeks. As she ate the mixed grill, followed by a lemon meringue tart, she realized that she had regained her sense of taste. She drank a glass of claret which David pressed upon her, and a faint colour came into her cheeks.

After the meal David showed her the contract which Graham Bernard had sent him, and Pearl told him it was fair enough and said he should sign it and return it without delay. A new and heady excitement stirred in him as he realized he would see the play produced in the autumn, and that if it did well it would be transferred to the Corinthian. More wonderful than that even was the knowledge that Pearl would be with him.

Weeks ago when he had first met her, she seemed sure and triumphant, but now she was sad and wistful and, oddly, seemed even more attractive. He felt that she was suffering more than a normal unhappiness where Rose was concerned. Something was nagging at her, tormenting her, but he instinctively knew that it would be a mistake to question her. She needed trust, and that he could give her.

It was difficult for him to think dispassionately about Miles. Rose had told him that he was cold to Pearl, who none the less adored him. Rose, and occasionally Pearl herself, had hinted at some kind of mystery in their relationship. He decided that the sooner he got her away, the better. In some subtle fashion, her father was destroying her, and the less she saw of him the better.

He would have to be patient and strong, David thought, but a new confidence now inspired him. He could be both because he loved her so much. He had a new life to offer her; a life which would be valuable and sweet, and a devotion which would be unswerving. But to protest that here and now would be of little use. She must discover it for herself.

When the play contract had been signed and put in an envelope ready to post to Graham Bernard, they sat together by the fire. She leaning back in the big chair, he on the floor at her feet. Sometimes he kissed the hand which rested against his neck, and they talked in broken snatches. It was peaceful and beautiful, David thought, as the rest of their lives would be.

❋ CHAPTER 20 ❋

Emmeline Thorpe arrived two days later in a state of bustling confusion. She had decided to stay at the local hotel because, as she confided to Pearl, she really couldn't sleep in poor, dear Rose's room, in which everything had been left as it was when she was alive.

Kate seemed relieved at her decision. She told Pearl that when she returned from Hampshire she would herself attend to her darling girl's belongings. She would be strong enough then, and she would be happier to think that nobody else touched anything of Rose's. She told Pearl to lock the door of the room, and give her the key.

It was the first initiative she had shown, and Pearl was glad of it. Kate was on the way to recovery, and needed her less.

Emmeline's presence seemed to act as a tonic. The sisters gossiped about mutual acquaintances, talked of their childhood and drank innumerable cups of tea. Later in the day, Kate went for a short walk, leaning on Emmeline's arm.

New interests would spring up in Kate's life, Pearl thankfully realized. She was absorbed when Emmeline talked of her children and Emmeline hinted that her oldest boy, who was just leaving school, had a fine business head and would think himself on the road to fortune if Miles would take him on at the factory.

That, thought Pearl, might be a very good thing for Miles and Kate. There would be young life about the place, for if Miles did give the boy a trial, he would naturally live with his uncle and aunt. In time he might become almost a son to them.

Neither Kate nor Emmeline paid much attention to Pearl that day and she had time to herself in which to finish her packing, and to write the letter which would be found after she left Brightwell.

Careless now if they were seen lunching together, she and David had a meeting in Northpond and made their plans. Nothing could go wrong now, thought Pearl, but yet she had the sense of treading on crumbling ground.

Towards Miles her heart was hard. She never wanted to see him again, and no doubt he would be glad to see the last of her. Always there had been an abyss between them. Sometimes it had been precariously bridged, but his treatment of her during the last few weeks had made it impossible that it would ever be bridged again.

There could be no explanations now, and no tardy reconciliation. She was out of his power and he was out of hers. She could not hurt him or punish him. The relationship between them had snapped abruptly without any final scene or desperate parting. It was better that way, and yet Pearl knew there would be aching memories. Always she would think of Miles as he had been these last weeks; his eyes cold, his hand refusing to touch hers, his manifest effort to even speak to her.

It was late now, and the silence pressed upon her. She lay on her bed, ready dressed, with her eyes fixed on the clock. She was very tired and she slept for a few minutes, to awake with a start and to look again at the clock. Supposing she had let the appointed time pass, and David, waiting to be admitted, had gone away.

Nobody stirred. Miles had gone to bed early saying he was tired, as well he might be by the unceasing flow of Emmeline's conversation; and Kate always slept heavily, due to the sleeping tablets which the doctor prescribed.

In the living-room the curtains had not been pulled across the windows, and as the moon was full it was almost as light as day. Pearl set down her suitcase and opened one of the windows. She had put on her hat and coat before she walked softly down the passage. At the open window, she whistled; a bird's note, and an answering note came to her.

It was the pre-arranged signal, and a few minutes later, David was outside. She stood aside for him to enter and spoke in a low voice. 'We must be quiet. I don't think either Miles or Kate are awake, but there's the chance.'

'Yes.' David put his arm around her and held her close. He said : 'Did you leave a letter?'

'Yes. Did you?'

He nodded, then turned her face to his and found her lips. Her body was taut in his arms, and he sensed her nervous tension, that something of her mind or heart or spirit which still instinctively withdrew from him.

'Kate will be all right,' said Pearl, as though answering an unspoken question. 'Her sister came today and it did her good to see her. I wrote that you were driving me to London as you had decided to try your luck there. What did you say in your letter to your father?'

'Much the same. They will suspect, Pearl . . .'

'That there is something between us. Yes, I suppose so, but they can't be sure, and there's nothing we can do about it.'

'I told Reevy,' said David. 'She's glad for us, though she will miss me. I promised we would have her for a visit as soon as we could.'

'She's been so decent about everything.' Pearl hesitated, and then said : 'David, there's one thing – you won't be silly about money, will you? I have enough, and a house. We must share it.'

He smiled : 'I promise you I won't be unreasonably proud, but I've saved enough to keep me going for some time. I had to save when – when I thought we should be living here. Rose and I . . . buying a house and furnishing it.'

'Of course.' Pearl moved away from him. 'She wanted that so much. I'm illogical. I wish she could have had it, and that we could still have everything too.'

He said : 'Don't let's talk of it – not now. We shan't for-

133

get her. It would be impossible; but try not to remember tonight. We ought to be going, darling. There's no reason to wait.' He saw her case and picked it up : 'Is this all you are taking?'

'Yes. I've left my trunk packed, and in my letter to Father, I asked him to have it sent on to me.'

'The car's at the end of the road.'

David moved to the window, with Pearl about to follow him. Then he heard her gasp, as though with fear. Instantly he swung around and saw the door open, saw Miles in his dressing-gown standing there.

A strange wave of excitement swept over Pearl. So it wasn't to be easy after all; not a silent escape without pain or argument. It was to end in the combat which was more appropriate.

But David was furious to be trapped at the last minute. He set down the suitcase and faced Miles, realizing as he gazed at that ageing but still handsome face how much he disliked him.

'So you are leaving us?' said Miles.

'Were you in the kitchen all the time?' Pearl asked coolly.

'I was. I heard your voices though not what you were saying. I'd got up to find the book I'd been reading, as I was unable to sleep, and then I remembered I had had no supper and I was making a sandwich when I heard your voices. Couldn't you have gone in the morning?'

'It seemed easier this way,' explained David.

Miles sat down on the arm of an easy chair and surveyed them. His manner was leisurely, and now he had the advantage of his years. His slight and superior smile suggested they were both rather ridiculous.

'Somewhat obviously romantic, isn't it?' he enquired.

Pearl realized the mocking tone must be maddening to David, though it did not affect her. Pleasure mingled with the odd excitement. At least her last memory of Miles would not be of his sullen face avoiding her, of his impenetrable silence bruising her. 'It isn't an elopement,' she said.

David made a movement of protest, but before he could speak she put out her hand in a quieting gesture : 'Please, David . . .'

'You are going off together,' said Miles.

'I left a letter in my room, explaining. Kate has her sister and no longer needs me.'

Despite Pearl's restraining hand, David cut in : 'It's been too much for both of us. You don't realize what a strain this has been to Pearl. She would break if she had much more of it – the nursing, the constant companionship. Now Mrs Shandon has her sister and no longer needs her, as Pearl has just said.'

Miles looked him over reflectively. His gaze expressed a mild contempt, but he was forced to admit that David had changed; there was a new assurance; a new pride and confidence.

'So you are throwing over your position here?' he asked.

'I have to. I told you and my father I was not cut out for it, but for Rose's sake . . .'

'She tried to make something of you.'

'And it was because of her I tried to make a go of it,' David retorted. 'I'd have got along somehow if she had lived, but now – it's hopeless, and I don't propose to sacrifice the rest of my life to a job that means nothing to me.'

'You may be right.' The indifference of Miles's voice was a quiet insult. 'Speaking for myself I'd say you are a dead loss anyhow, but your father will find it a blow.'

'Yes – I'm sorry.'

That was not altogether perfunctory. David owed little to Joseph Page, but now, loving Pearl as he did, he could better understand him. Real life had finished for his father when his mother had died. He had been able to exist only by retreating into a world of his own.

'I can't stop you going,' said Miles, his glance leaving David to rest upon Pearl, 'but before you do, there are one or two things I ought to tell you.'

'Father !' Pearl exclaimed.

This was it then, she thought. This was real danger. Miles would destroy her if he could. And he so easily might. She had not yet decided how much or how little she would tell David, but she did know that confidences would not be forced from her and that she could choose her own time for them. But Miles would give his merciless version of her character and her actions, here and now, and the imperfect truth of his conclusions would be veiled by his certainty.

At the least David would be hurt and shaken, and that she would not allow. He should not be forced into defending her to her own father, for defend her he would, even though Miles succeeded in implanting the seeds of poison.

'Well, my dear,' said Miles.

'I want to talk to you alone.'

'But you were going away without doing so.'

'Yes, I was. As David says, it was easier that way; but now that you have found out it's different. There are things I want to say, and you must listen to me.'

After a moment, Miles made a gesture of assent. 'Very well, I will do that.'

'David, will you wait for me in the car?' Pearl asked. 'Come back for me in half an hour, if I'm not with you by then.'

David regarded her doubtfully. She was no longer wistful and pliable. She had shaken off her weariness. If there was to be conflict between herself and Miles, she would now welcome it. There was that between them which would have been unresolved for ever had they departed in silence; something which might have become an aching frustration to her. Although to leave her might mean that he ran the risk of losing her, David knew he must let her have her way.

'If you insist,' he said reluctantly.

'Don't be afraid. I shan't weaken.' Pearl smiled at him.

He nodded. He had said he trusted her, and he did. 'Half an hour then,' he said, and went out by the long window.

❉ CHAPTER 21 ❉

Miles said: 'If I am to hold my tongue, you will have to think up some convincing arguments in the next half-hour.'

The next half-hour, thought Pearl, would be worse for David than for her. He would be waiting impatiently, anxiously, in the dark, counting the minutes as they passed; but she was able to fight and the prospect of it stimulated her.

Hate could be near to love, and sometimes it was more satisfying. Certainly she hated Miles now. She was out in the open, prepared for battle, and however much he might wound her, she would wound him in an even deadlier way.

'Well, go ahead,' Miles encouraged. 'You're the chief witness for the defence.'

'The case for the prosecution is weak,' Pearl observed.

'There is a case for all that.'

Pearl sat down on the sofa. She said: 'For myself I don't care, but why heap more horror on David? He's taken enough. He's decent. He intended to marry Rose whatever happened. He was prepared to give up everything for her; me as well as the work which meant so much to him, the work he can do.'

'I gather that you are in love with each other,' said Miles.

'Yes, we are.'

'Did Rose know?'

'She had no idea of it.'

'So you had a very good reason for wanting her out of the way. I admit I was puzzled. The charm motive, even though you might believe that it had mystic power, was a bit too outlandish, even for you.'

'Do you really suspect me of killing her? David would be horrified to think you could accuse me.'

'He should be warned. He's not a bad chap, and his father and I have been friends for many years. I owe it to him, to put things before him.'

'About my mother perhaps. I always knew you would think it your duty to tell anyone who might want to marry me that I am a Eurasian; and under ordinary circumstances I shouldn't have tried to prevent you, because if that influenced a man I loved, I shouldn't want him any longer.'

'In this instance I'm not considering your mother.'

'Then we can dispense with that aspect, although actually my mixed blood is no concern of David's, for I've no intention of marrying him.'

'He thinks you have.'

'Because he loves me, he expects to prevail over me, but I've been honest with him. I've told him I won't marry him or anyone. I love him, and I'll live with him if he'll have me, but not marriage . . .'

'By the time I have talked to him he will need temerity to take you on in any role,' Miles said. 'He'll probably feel that life with a cobra would be less risky.' And then as Pearl made no reply to this calculated brutality, Miles said with a voice on the verge of breaking : 'Tell me the truth, damn you. It's hell not to know.'

'Suppose there *is* nothing to know?'

'I've seen guilt in your eyes over and over again.'

'Really? Yet I flattered myself that I was a puzzle to you.'

'Would you go off like this, in the night, if you had a clear conscience?'

'I don't see why not? I shall enjoy driving through the night with David.'

'And with no thought of the shock it will be to Kate when she finds you gone?'

'You can think up something to tell her. She will soon be leaving with her sister, and she doesn't need me now Emmeline is here. Anyway, I should have gone when she left, for I wouldn't stay here with you – alone. How could I? After all, you did nearly strangle me.'

'I was half out of my mind. I'd had enough that day to send me crazy.'

'It seems,' said Pearl bitterly, 'as though there's a tendency in both of us to liquidate people.'

'Now you're deliberately torturing me,' Miles accused.

'Haven't you tortured me? Ever since Rose died you've avoided me, you've been sick with loathing of me. Days passed and you did not speak to me.'

'What had we to say to each other that could be said?'

'It seems that we're saying it now. You've hated to sit down to a meal with me, hated to be in the same room with me. Kate, in her misery turned to me, and you even hated me for that, though I did all I could for her. In your heart you've judged and condemned me.'

He was silent, not denying it, but there was agony in his eyes and she turned away her own, in order not to see him thus, not to pity him and so weaken. She said : 'How do you think I killed Rose?'

'I don't know – how can I know?'

'You must have some theory.'

If he had it was a theory which he had not clearly defined and he said stumblingly : 'Red Rocks cove is a quiet place where few people go, but she liked to swim there, and you often rowed out there. You could have been there that day; you could have quarrelled.'

Pearl had long since decided that she would never admit to Miles or to anyone else that she and Rose had met on the day of her death, for then she would be questioned and nobody could say what suspicions might not be aroused. With Miles it would be more than suspicion, it would be the confirmation of his worst fears.

'And what did I do then?' she enquired scornfully. 'Did I club Rose over the head with an oar and pitch her into the sea? I should have had to be strong, she was quite a hefty girl, besides, there wasn't a mark on her.'

'I've told you I don't know how it was done, but you have the charm she was wearing before she left home. Therefore it stands to reason you were with her.'

'I've told you I found it.'

'Very convenient,' Miles sneered.

But she might be able to convince him of that, Pearl thought. She might, if she employed sincerity, gentleness and good-will, convince him of many things. Perversely she had no intention of so doing. It suited her to hurt him, not to set his mind at rest. The more she tormented him, the greater her acrid satisfaction. She looked at him consideringly, and said : 'Suppose I reconstruct the scene for you.'

'Do you mean – how it was?'

Ah, that was the right line to take, gloated Pearl's demon. It was not she who was in his power, but he who was in hers. If he ruined her chance of happiness with David, it would be only after she had made it impossible for him to know another peaceful moment.

'You can judge for yourself.'

Pearl rose from the sofa and started to walk about the room. She spoke quietly, without dramatic emphasis : 'It was a lovely day – warm, sunny. On the sea there wasn't a soul to be seen; no bathers, no other boats. I was happy. I thought how peaceful and satisfying it was – the aloneness – and how hateful it would be when the tourist season started. Then I saw Rose; she was swimming. I was annoyed and hoped she wouldn't come near me; we weren't on good terms. I wanted to forget she was there, so I didn't watch her. Then I heard her call out – my name.'

She paused, a studied pause. Miles's intent eyes were fixed on her. 'Well, go on,' he said, when the prolonged silence was beyond his endurance.

But Pearl was in no hurry to end his unrest. She stood by the centre table, playing idly with some flowers in a bowl there. She removed a dead flower, rearranged the others, and then continued in a leisurely voice : 'She had stopped swimming, was in difficulty of some kind. I remembered her other attack of cramp. I started to row towards her and saw her sink. She was wearing a yellow bathing-cap and it disappeared. I wondered what I had better do.'

'You should have swam out to her – helped her.'

'I'm not a strong swimmer. She might have dragged me under.'

'What *did* you do?' Miles cried in an anguished voice.

'Waited. I knew she would come up again. It could have been less than a minute, but a dozen thoughts rushed through my mind. It's said they do when people are drowning, but it was Rose drowning – not I. I thought of how I loved David, and how he loved me. I thought of how he was resolved to make up his quarrel with her, to give in to her. I thought of how much better off he would be without her, and of how happy I could make him.'

'Oh God, you let her drown !' Miles exclaimed.

Pearl stood at the back of the chair opposite to him, her arms folded on its back, her face inscrutable. She went on in her muted voice : 'She came to the surface again; she was conscious and she looked at me. The boat was very near, and she hadn't a doubt that I would help her. I saw the relief in her eyes, and the chain and the charm around her neck. I stretched out my arm, and she thought I was going to pull her towards me, but instead I pulled at the chain and tore it off. It was quite easy for the clasp was weak. Then I rowed away, and I closed my eyes. When I opened them I couldn't see her any more.'

She stopped and the silence was absolute. A smile flickered

on Pearl's face, as Miles gazed at her with horrified repulsion.

'Is this true?' he asked hoarsely.

'It could be.' Her voice was no longer serious, but flippant. 'Isn't it the sort of thing my mother might have done if she had wanted another woman out of the way?'

'I'm asking you. Is this a confession?'

'No. It's what is called a hypothetical case. Quite a convincing one, isn't it?'

Despair was added to Miles's sense of revulsion. He suspected now that she was deriving pleasure from this ghastly conflict. 'Pearl, do you hate me?' he asked.

'The odd thing would be if I didn't hate you.'

'I shielded you,' said Miles defensively. 'There might have been a different verdict at the inquest had I told all I knew, and all I suspected.'

'But it would have shown you up in a very unsympathetic light. After all, I am your daughter. Besides, think of the publicity. Newspaper reporters would have delved into the past, and found out all about your first marriage.'

With a spring, Miles was out of his chair, had covered the space between them. 'Take that smile off your face,' he roared. 'How dare you mock me? You're telling the truth as likely as not, though at the same time you're pretending that it's a lie . . .'

Pearl retreated from him, holding up her hands to ward him off : 'Keep your distance,' she said. 'Last time we came to grips, I had a sore throat for a week.'

That brought Miles to a standstill, as she had known it would. He said sullenly : 'I've been punished enough for that — for a moment's loss of self-control.'

'Some men have been punished on the gallows,' she reminded him, 'though I can forgive you for that . . . it's for other things . . .'

'I neglected you when you were a child. Is that what you mean?'

'It wasn't neglect — it was worse. You loved me unwillingly. You were never natural with me. Any small fault of mine was magnified into evil. You probed — expecting to find my mother in me, and you still do. Yet she was obedient to you; faithful, loving.'

'I've told you so,' said Miles.

'But she was your unforgettable mistake, wasn't she, and my existence was a calamity? What a fool you have been – twice over, unable to value all we had to give. Has Kate ever treated you as though you were lord of all her world?'

'Kate,' said Miles aloofly, 'has always had a loyal affection for me, and I for her. I know where I am with Kate.'

The old stock phrase! At another time Pearl could have laughed, but she was obsessed by the way he had wronged her, and there was no laughter, only a vibrating anger.

'And didn't you know where you were with me?' she said. 'Didn't you know you were the reason for living? I was clever and glad of it, hoping you would be proud. I was beautiful, and thought you would take pleasure in me; I made myself fond of Kate and Rose because they were part of you, and I thought if they liked and trusted me, that you would also trust me. But it was no use. I threw a knife at Rose when I was a child, and since then you've expected me to stick a second knife in her heart.'

'Wasn't I right to fear it? Rose is dead. Have you shed a tear for her? Have you grieved for her?'

Had she not? But he would never know how much! She said : 'Make allowances for my Oriental stoicism. One grieves for suffering, for pain; not for release.'

'Release!' cried Miles. 'Who wants release from life at Rose's age? She was happy before you came here. Even when she was unhappy, she could have had no wish to die.'

'How can you tell? I've wished myself dead many times.'

That statement struck at Miles's heart. He wavered, knowing his guilt, and for an instant he saw Pearl clearly, not as the incarnation of evil, but as his lovely child, grown into a lovely woman, wounded by him beyond healing. But almost instantly his heart hardened.

'There was nothing morbid about Rose,' he said.

'Morbid or not, she could have gone out that day determined to die. If you reflect, it was all rather mysterious. She told you she was to meet David, was going swimming with him. She said they would probably spend the evening together, that you were not to worry if she was late coming home. But she knew she had no intention of meeting him.'

'David explained that. It was because she was unhappy and wanted to get away from us for a while; because she knew her mother suspected all was not well and had questioned her.'

'Yes, I know that's David's theory,' said Pearl.

'And a reasonable one.'

'So are other theories. That she no longer wanted to live seems reasonable enough to me. She hoped her death would be written off as an accident – and it was at the inquest. She knew you would remember she had once had cramp, which would account for it.'

'If she wanted to die, it must have been because you had taken her lover from her,' said Miles heavily.

Pearl shook her head. 'Oh no, she never guessed it. It was I who urged her to go to London with David, to live his life, rather than insist that he should live hers. That way she could have been happy.'

Miles made a gesture of dissent. He paced the room while Pearl watched him with the absolute stillness which from time to time had struck both Kate and Rose as unusual and fascinating.

'Never,' said Miles, 'not after having so disappointed us.'

'Then if she was so miserable, so bewildered, would it be strange if she swam too far out to sea, deliberately, until she was exhausted and had not the strength to return? The sea was so blue and calm and kind. It must have been a temptation to let go; to sink into it, for ever.'

Miles stopped abruptly in his restless pacing. He said: 'Rose was a good girl. Suicide is a sin; it's criminal weakness. She was incapable of it.'

Weakness? Pearl wondered. In her mind there was doubt. Did it not need courage of a singular kind to take that leap into the unknown, to thrust forward into the illimitable before one's appointed time?

'You may be right,' she said. 'She was your daughter. You may have understood *her*.'

'I did,' said Miles positively.

'Not suicide then?'

'I'll never believe it. It would have been out of character.'

'But not out of character for me to have killed her? You

can believe that?'

'Yes, God forgive me, I can.'

Unexpected tears stung Pearl's eyes. She fought them, resolved that they would not flow down her cheeks. Miles, sitting with his hands covering his eyes, and his shoulders bowed, looked like an old man. The foolish, devoted child who had once been herself had loved him so, had been so proud of his good looks, his height, his breadth of shoulder. Her father – and they belonged to each other; the most wonderful person in the world to her childish fancy. Later, when she had grown to womanhood, and Cynthia had laughed at her, mercilessly exposing Miles's triteness, his commonplace qualities, Pearl, though she had intellectually agreed, had not agreed emotionally. Now, in revenge, she had brought him low. But he deserved it. She was avenging her wrongs, and perhaps also the wrongs of the girl who had been her mother.

Looking up at last, Miles said: 'Let us go back to your hypothetical case – that you were near the red rocks and that Rose swam out there, and drowned because you refused to help her. Suppose you were seen near that spot by someone who kept quiet about it, who did not come forward to give evidence?'

Pearl's eyes opened wide. In them Miles discerned, or thought he discerned apprehension, as she said quickly: 'That's not possible. The place was deserted.'

'How do you know, if you were not there?'

A false move! Though she recovered herself quickly, Pearl knew it was hopeless to try to cover up her blunder. With a shrug, she sat down in the chair, against which she had been leaning. 'You think you've caught me out,' she said coolly.

'And haven't I? According to your story at the inquest you rowed in the opposite direction. Why did you lie about that?'

'Because I wasn't there at the time which mattered. I was far out at sea. When did this person see me near the red rocks?'

'Nobody saw you as far as I know,' Miles admitted.

'It was a trap. I might have known it. But it doesn't prove anything.'

144

'It proves,' said Miles, 'that you are not to be believed; that you are a liar, that you could be . . .'

'A murderess? Well, say it — say it . . .'

'I do say it.'

There was pure hatred now, unmixed with truth, in the glance which flashed between them, and a keen desire to mortally wound in Pearl's low and controlled voice as she said: 'But at the worst I didn't actually kill her. Isn't it Shakespeare who wrote: *"Thou shalt not kill; but needs not strive officiously to keep alive."* '

· To Miles this was confirmation indeed, and only now did he truly realize how much he had longed to be convinced of error. He cried out in a broken voice: 'Oh God, my poor girl — struggling there, praying to you for help.'

'I've made no confession,' Pearl pointed out.

Exposed now in all his weakness, Miles involuntarily stretched out a hand to her: 'Why don't you?' he said pleadingly. 'Why not put an end to all this? It would be quite safe. There's nobody but me to hear you. It would relieve your mind.'

'You mean it would end the suspense and relieve yours.'

'And you deny me because you hate me. I deserve it, perhaps, though with it all, I can't bring myself to hate you.'

'Why should you? I am what you have made me.'

Miles's heavy sigh was nearer to a groan. He said: 'We are too close to each other for hate.'

'As close as a hair shirt,' she agreed.

Bitterness ebbed and flowed. There was too much feeling, too much emotion, she thought. She wanted to be as cold and as sure as steel, but with her divided mind it was impossible. If she was tearing him in bits, she was also tearing herself. If he was weak, she also was aware of weakness. Weariness was seeping over her, and the longing to weep. Conscious of her growing exhaustion, as he, too, must also be conscious of it, she said: 'I may be harmless enough. Consider. I've fitted in with all your friends here. They like me, and it's difficult for a woman to deceive another woman for any length of time. They think me a nice, quiet girl; helpful and sympathetic. Your monstrous conception of me could be no more than a bogey which you have invented.'

'I wish it were,' said Miles.

145

This couldn't go on, thought Pearl. They would have to end it one way or the other. She said: 'You've got yourself into a frightful muddle, and why should I try to pull you out of it? There's another theory, though, if you could accept it.'

'Go on,' said Miles, in a voice as weary as hers.

'Isn't it possible I told you the truth – that I found the charm, and that I hadn't the remotest idea of what had happened to Rose until I heard people talking? Then I came home as quickly as possible, praying it might not be true, hoping to find her here. There was moonlight, remember, and as I came up the garden path I saw something glittering on the hawthorn bush which is overgrown and which we talked of having cut back. Tangled in the branches was Rose's bronze charm on its gold chain, and I pulled it out. The clasp was broken. It should have been properly mended, but Rose had forgotten about it. As she went down the path, it could have fallen from her neck, could have caught on a branch of the bush. It would have been natural enough had nobody else seen it.'

'But David and I went down that path on our way to the shore,' Miles objected.

'The moonlight happened to shine on it as I passed. The clasp is broken; see for yourself.'

Pearl, as she spoke, took the charm on its chain from her pocket, handed it over to Miles and watched him examine it. He said: 'It would have been broken, if you had torn it from her neck.'

'You would rather believe that,' she said, and bit her lips to stop them trembling.

'No – I would give anything, all I possess, to be convinced you are innocent. What is there left if I can't believe in you? Against my better judgement I twice brought you and Rose together, and it meant disaster for her. That was my responsibility.'

'She could have had an attack of cramp and drowned if I had been in Australia. Nothing but a perfect alibi would satisfy you, and as I was by myself all day, I can't provide one.'

'I've never understood you,' said Miles.

'You tried too hard.' Pearl sighed. 'Did you ever treat

146

Kate or Rose as dark mysteries? As Kate said, you always behaved to me as though I was different, but I'm not, you know,
though sometimes the egoist in me thought I was, and I
played up. Often I forgot and felt as ordinary as anyone else,
though we are none of us really ordinary. If you had delved
into Rose's mind, you might have unearthed impulses and de-
sires which would have surprised you.'

'Nonsense! She was entirely open and straightforward.'

'Then she must have been even more uninteresting than she
appeared. But don't think I despised her simplicity. It was her
selfishness and obstinacy which antagonized me. If you weren't
so biased I could show you . . . but what's the use of trying?
Nothing would convince you that I'm not subtle and devious.
Oh, you fool! Don't you see? If I couldn't be loved and
trusted, it was something to have you afraid of me, fascinated
by me.'

And now she thought, now at last, she had revealed herself,
but he wouldn't or couldn't accept it; for he was entrenched
in his obstinate blindness, the victim of his own conviction,
his text-book certainty that because of her mixed blood she
was inherently unstable.

'You're very plausible,' said Miles.

Well, she had expected it, and she was at the end of all
effort. Plausible was his favourite word as applied to her. She
stood beside him and put out her hand for the charm which he
still held.

'Take it,' said Miles and repressed a shudder. 'There's
something horrible about it.'

'No – it's very interesting, something to dream about. I
wonder how many other women have cherished it down
through the years. I wonder what they were like – if they were
good or evil. I wonder if anyone ever took it from a dead neck
to hang around her own.'

'You believe it has some magic power.'

He could believe that of her. It was part of his case
against her that she was savagely superstitious, and Pearl knew
what he was thinking, knew that it would take a miracle to
eradicate such a belief. She said : 'Not really. It attracts me
because it's so old; because the sun god is the symbol of light
and truth.'

'It brought no good fortune to Rose.'

147

'Poor Rose,' said Pearl, with an unexpected gentleness. 'And yet how can we tell? Perhaps it is only now that she knows what real happiness is Perhaps her only sorrow is this conflict between us.'

It struck Miles that for the first time there was true sadness for a dead girl in her expression. He said slowly : 'You said that sincerely.'

Instantly both pity and sorrow were obliterated by mockery; perhaps of him, perhaps of herself. Sitting on the arm of the sofa she said lightly : 'Ah! But I'm a good actress, and that's quite a telling line.'

'Haven't you baited me enough?' demanded Miles. 'One thing at least is positive – the streak of cruelty in you.'

'All women can be cruel when they have been hurt. Of course I have said cruel things to you tonight; things I have wanted to say for years. They are all true, and I don't regret them.'

She was not the type to regret, thought Miles, but if he had accused her of a crime of which she was innocent, she had had a right to say all and more than all that she had said. A new sense of horror smote him; but now it was horror of himself. If he was wrong, as he could be wrong, what ghastly and unnatural injustice he had dealt out to her. He said with an effort : 'With all my soul I regret having hurt you, having made you what you are.'

'So evil?'

'So bitter. Cynthia warned me. She thought me ignoble. She said that one day you would despise me and no longer care.'

Rising, he stood beside her, and for an instant his hand rested on her shoulder. Pearl had been gazing at the charm in the palm of her hand, but now she slipped it into her coat pocket and looked up at him gravely, though with an ironical gleam in her eyes.

'Aunt Cynthia had great insight,' she remarked.

'I should have devoted myself to you, I suppose – not married again.'

'Nobody could have expected you to sacrifice all your life to a memory,' Pearl said. 'You could have married Kate, and still have been proud of my mother and of me. But I am proud of her, Father. I always have been. I like to think of

148

her proud and ancient race, of her illustrious birth, of her courage and her virtue . . . I like . . .'

She broke off as David tapped on the window, and Miles looked towards it. Their duel was over, and who could say which of them had won? The fight had gone out of them both, and with a deadly weariness, Pearl told herself that it had all been futile. Suspicion and anger and pain still possessed them, but they had come to an impasse.

'The half-hour is over,' she said quietly. 'Let him in. Tell him whatever you choose.'

✳ CHAPTER 22 ✳

Miles went to the window and opened it, and as David came in, he looked from one to the other. At once he was struck by Pearl's excessive pallor. She looked, he thought, as though half the life had been drained out of her. He could imagine how it had been; threats and pleas and exhortations on Miles's part. She had resisted them, but they had brought her near to collapse.

'Well,' he said, his eyes fixed on Miles.

But it was Pearl who answered him, as she dragged herself to her feet. She said tonelessly : 'I'm ready.' Tonelessly, but there was challenge in the two words, and she straightened her shoulders as though with pride.

'What about your father?' David asked.

'Oh yes, there was something he wanted to tell you. Was it important, Father?'

Her heart had started to pound. It was battering against her side. She waited, and in her pride she would not look at Miles, would not try to influence him with any prayerful glance. And then after an agonizing pause came Miles's voice; slow and heavy. 'I thought so at the time, but now . . .'

David broke in impatiently. He must get Pearl out of this place as soon as possible. She had taken all she could take.

'Go ahead,' he said. 'I'm prepared for anything you may have to say. You can't have much of an opinion of me. I'm clearing out, which will be a blow to my father. I fell in love with Pearl when I was engaged to her sister, though I swear Rose would never have known of it, and I should have tried to make her happy.'

'That's all in the past, and I'm not your judge,' said Miles, and heard Pearl's smothered gasp.

But relief came to him as he spoke, for this indeed was the truth, and one which he should have recognized long ago. Whatever Pearl had done or had not done, justice or revenge was not for him — her father. He could not betray her — if there was anything to betray. For what he considered the misfortune of her birth, she was not responsible, and had his love for her been faultless, suspicion of her would never have entered his mind. He would have accepted her explanation, would have believed without question that she had come upon the bronze disc by accident, and if guilt was hers his absolute trust might have softened her.

But as it was, his denial of love and his doubt of her had brought their own punishment. That she had loved him he could not doubt, and even if it had been a twisted love, his understanding might have perfected it.

'But you must feel sore enough,' said David.

'Forget it,' Miles answered wearily. 'You and Pearl care for one another, it seems. I'd prefer not to go into that . . . she's a woman, and what she chooses to do in the future is her own business. She probably understands you better than you understand her, but if you can win her confidence much may depend upon it.'

Further than that he could not go, for he was aware of his helplessness. Pearl would marry David, or she would evade marrying him, whatever his counsel might be. She had no respect for his judgement or advice, and could he wonder at it?

'I know there's some mystery,' said David, and was unwillingly sorry for Miles, seeing his haggard face. 'It sticks out a mile, but it doesn't concern me. Pearl can tell me if she wants to, or she can keep it to herself. I shan't question her. It's what she is that concerns me, and I know what she is.'

'Oh, you do, eh?'

Pearl heard the irony in his voice if David did not. The

young, obtuse fool, thought Miles. Pearl might love him with her body, but her mind and spirit would be for ever beyond his comprehension.

'Certainly I know her,' said David. 'Character speaks for itself. Pearl wouldn't let Rose suffer. She gave up years of her life to nurse her aunt; she's had a hard time with Mrs Shandon these last few weeks. Don't these things speak for her; don't they mean charity and pity and generosity?'

'Perhaps,' said Pearl lightly, 'I enjoy being a martyr.'

David smiled at her, moved to her, and put his arm round her. 'Not you. You love life too well. Of course you're not always as sensible as you might be, for instance there's this crack-pot notion about not wanting to marry.'

'She told you that?' asked Miles with surprise.

'Flaunted it at me – told me it was not for her, and that I could take it or leave it. I didn't pester her. It was enough for me to have her care for me. So long as she did there wasn't much to worry about. But don't be afraid, Mr Shandon, I shan't – I mean I won't – you can trust me.'

Miles stared at him with amazement, and Pearl uttered a half-choked laugh; but she was proud of him for the single-minded, trustful love which to him seemed the only worth-while way of loving.

Answering the look she bent on him, which was deep and loving and tenderly amused, David said : 'I understand you better than your father imagines, better than he does himself, most likely.'

'I hope you are right,' said Miles.

And by some freak of insight he could be right. Miles, in admitting it, achieved an unprecedented humility which brought with it a glimmer of hope. Such confidence, if justified, might be the one solution. Where he had wounded, David would heal. Where he had lacked justice, David would console by faith.

'We ought to wait longer, perhaps,' said David, 'but Pearl hasn't any real place here, and neither have I.'

'Well, if that is so, if that's what you think, you had better be on your way.'

To Pearl, it was the order of release. She could go. She had nothing more to fear. Miles had set her free, and David would accept her with joy and without questioning. She said, half dazed : 'There's my case, David.'

David stooped to pick it up. With his free arm still en-
folding her, he led her towards the window. She was so tired
that she sagged against him.

'Goodbye, sir,' said David. 'I shall write, we shall both
write.'

But as they were about to step out into the night, Pearl
pulled away. She said : 'There's my coat, I'd forgotten it, and
I shall need it. Go on ahead, David, take my case. I shall be
with you in a minute.'

He obeyed her unsuspectingly, and once more she was alone
with Miles. Tears misted her eyes.

'Where is your coat?' Miles asked.

'It's hanging in the hall.' She could scarcely utter the
words.

As she went out she looked around her at a room which
had suddenly become friendly, which for all its uninspired
taste had for a time been her home. Then Miles returned
with the coat and held it out, waiting to help her on with it.
Not speaking, Pearl slipped her arms into the sleeves, and
then, suddenly, she twisted around and clung to him. Hate was
dead, and pride was vanquished. In the end he had given her
all he could give.

'Father – thank you, Father,' she whispered.

Tears fell upon her cheeks and sobs caught her breath.
Miles held her closely, his lips against her hair. 'He's waiting
for you,' he said. 'Take care of yourself. That boy – I wish
. . .'

'That I am what he believes me to be. What can I say?'

'Nothing – say nothing.'

Words could not mend the past, and only love, a different
kind of love, which he must teach himself to learn, could
give him any part in her future. She raised her face and he
kissed her.

'I love you, Father,' Pearl said, and still weeping, she tore
herself away from him and ran down the garden path.

CHAPTER 23

The little motor sped along the moon-drenched roads and Pearl sat close to David, not speaking and almost motionless. David was aware of a deep content. To him this was the first step along the road which they would tread together, and for now he asked for nothing more. He looked down upon Pearl's white face and saw that her eyes were closed. Just as well if she slept, he thought, she was completely exhausted. That she had gone through some gruelling experience that evening he did not doubt, but it was over, and now it was his job to take care of her.

The dark lashes which made tiny fans upon Pearl's cheeks were lifted and she looked up at him; a serious, testing gaze.

'I thought you were sleeping,' he said. 'I hoped you were.'

'I couldn't sleep – not yet. David, we have to talk. There are things which have to be said, things which I was afraid my father would say, and say wrongly.'

'Oh, my sweet, not tonight; there's all time before us, and you've had enough to take,' David protested, but when she did not answer, he slowed down, and brought the motor to a standstill in a quiet lane.

'Now,' he said, 'we can stop here if you're determined to talk, not that anything you can say will make any difference. I'd far rather you let it all ride, whatever it is, and we could have a moonlight picnic. Dear old Reevy packed some sandwiches and there's a bottle of sherry in the back. Drink a glass, darling. It will do you good.'

'Oh, very well,' Pearl assented.

David reached out a long arm to the back seat, and produced the sandwiches and the bottle of sherry and two glasses. They drank and ate, but when Pearl refused a second glass of sherry she broke the silence and said abruptly, because she was unable to think of any opening which would be other than abrupt : 'David, I'm not half-Spanish. I mean my mother wasn't a Spaniard.'

'No? Well, that did cross my mind once or twice, not that I bothered about it, but it struck me that your face, your beautiful face, was more Eastern than Southern European.'

'My mother – was dark – an Indian,' said Pearl painfully. 'She was – her father was the rajah of a small state. My father, after she died, was afraid to tell people, and few knew anything about her when she was alive because she died so soon after he brought her to England. He has always loved me, but he was afraid of what he had done in marrying my mother and having a child by her.'

David's arm tightened round her, while he sought for words which would be simple and satisfying. He had been prepared for a shock, but was not aware of any particular reaction except anger when he thought of Miles. Had he held this over Pearl's head as an unspoken threat?

'Do you mind – terribly?' she asked in a shaken voice.

'I don't mind in the least. I've told you I half suspected it, though I hadn't decided what nationality you were on your mother's side. I knew your father had travelled in China as well as in the European countries, and I once met a Manchu girl who slightly reminded me of you. What does it matter to us, my darling? I can see you think it does though, and I suppose that's why you have barred marriage.'

Pearl said : 'I'm a Eurasian, and I've heard English people say – and I've read in novels – that we are supposed to inherit the worst traits of our two nationalities.'

David did not believe this and said so. He kissed her, and felt her tears upon his lips, while in broken words she tried to tell him what her mother had meant to Miles in the way of allure and passion, though her racial traits had been repugnant to him. Although he had loved her to the end, it had been as one under a spell might have loved a witch.

'But I believe she was good,' Pearl said. 'What if she did want to avenge herself on a man who had tried to force himself upon her; it was only because she loved Father so much. I suppose she did remember something of the black magic she had seen practised when she was a child; those women, shut away in purdah, must have amused themselves in odd ways; tried to think they had power when they had none. But don't blame Father, perhaps any man in his position would have felt as he did; felt a horror which he also felt for me.'

'He was a fool,' said David.

'But you or anyone might have reacted in the same way.'

'No – not if there was real love. Your mother was scarcely more than a child; she hadn't grown up; neither was her sense of religion grown-up. If she believed so strongly in a personal devil, she should also believe in a personal God. A man who had a strong sense of the Godhead would have realized that for himself; he would have taught her love and mercy, and though they might have had difficult years, in the end their marriage would have been a success. It seems to me that under such conditions, such a marriage would have had more chance than many conventional ones.'

These were stumbling words, but they were sincere and they reached Pearl's heart. 'I don't know anything much about religion,' she said.

'Neither do I, but we will find out more together.'

That, he thought would be a necessity. Passion, desire they had, but it was the spiritual side of love they must cultivate. Though he had for a space seemed to be within touch of wisdom and strength, he was aware, as he held Pearl in his arms, of a frightening inadequacy.

'I'm no good at this sort of talk,' he said. 'I'm clumsy and I blunder, but it wasn't just chance which brought us together, nor chance that poor Rose died as she did.'

'No, not chance, but my father thinks or half thinks . . . that I was responsible for Rose's death. He accused me this evening, and I was cruel and taunted him, and would not deny it.'

The whole story was sobbed out brokenly, with her face against his shoulder, and he was thankful she did not see his appalled expression. There was poison here such as he had never imagined. She had suffered depths of pain and humiliation which horrified him. He realized with a sense of awe, but no shrinking, that his love would have to be great indeed to reach the depths of her tormented nature, and to heal the hurt of years.

'How could you think that anything less than marriage between us was possible?' he said, when at last her broken voice

155

was silent. 'My darling, don't you see, ours must be as perfect as we can make it. If we don't, it will mean destruction for both of us.'

'Yes – I see,' Pearl said. There was wonder in her heart now, and the first foretaste of peace, but there was still much to be told.

'I didn't kill Rose or watch her die,' she said, 'but I did see her that day, and I was cruel, as I am cruel so often. Rose found me at the red rocks and she was unhappy. After I had been speaking to her for a few minutes I knew that she had no idea you had decided to give in to her. I was so angry with her, and with you too, for throwing up so much that you valued – and so I didn't tell her. I thought it wouldn't do her any harm to suffer for a while longer. From something she said I imagined you were joining her, meeting her at the red rocks. I got into the boat I had moored and refused to take her with me. I told her to stay there on the sands and wait for you, as I preferred to be alone. If I had been kind and taken her with me, she wouldn't have drowned.'

'But how could you have known?' he asked.

'I didn't know. I thought you would soon be with her; that was one reason why I wanted to get away; so that I needn't see you. I was enraged with you both, but later . . . it seemed to me later there was a moment when I knew she was in danger. I was far out on the sea; much too far to be able to distinguish anyone on land, and I had been half asleep; but suddenly I was wide awake, and I had a sense – a sense of peril. I looked back at the land and the red rocks, and I thought I saw someone swimming beyond them. My reason couldn't believe it, and I couldn't be sure if I really did see a yellow bathing cap, the cap Rose always wore. But, David, if I had obeyed my instinct, the warning which came to me, if I had rowed back to be certain, I might have saved her. It wasn't because I wished her harm that I didn't, but because I was so certain I was being ridiculous. Even now I'm convinced it was impossible for me to see as far as I seemed to see. Afterwards I was haunted – I've dreamt about that moment over and over again – I've had a terrible sense of guilt.'

'It's been ghastly for you,' David said. 'But now you have told me it will be different, and I don't think you will dream that dream again.'

'If I had told Father he wouldn't have believed me. I couldn't tell him. I thought it would be just as impossible for you to believe me.'

'I shall always believe anything you tell me,' he said.

'Oh David!'

'That's true, Pearl.'

'I don't deserve you, I'm not worthy of you, though I'm not what Father has often feared I am. I've never had a lover, David, but only because I never met anyone I wanted. But I've pretended so much. Because Father thought me unscrupulous and mysterious, because it half-fascinated him and kept him always aware of me, I – in a way I encouraged him. I became hateful . . . oh darling, it might be better perhaps if we parted now.'

He pressed her closer to him. 'I shall never part with you. I love you, and apart from love, Rose's death would be quite meaningless if it did not help to bring us together.'

'But you can't think she died in order to give me happiness.'

'Not willingly, not consciously, but indirectly she did help us, Pearl, and I believe that changed as she must be now, she is glad of it; for if there is a future life, as I am convinced there is, she must already be much wiser than either you or I. Who can explain why you had that premonition of danger? It didn't help her, and it has brought misery to you, but I believe there was some very good reason for it. We have seen a tiny bit of an intricate pattern, and we can't make sense out of it in this life, but one day we shall.'

'Do you think I really saw her – swimming?'

David's thoughts were in such chaos that he would have found it impossible to say exactly what he did believe, but he replied firmly : 'That I am sure was an illusion, and you must put it out of your mind. Your father was to blame for that, and I dare say he knows it, but now you must learn to believe in yourself, as profoundly as I believe in you.'

'I had no idea you were like this.' Pearl spoke in a bewildered voice. 'I fell in love with you, and I thought it was because you were – rather sweet. I loved you for such silly reasons, because when you smiled it was more with your eyes than with your lips, because your voice was deep and kind. And then there was your talent, perhaps genius, but it was underdeveloped, and I wanted to help . . . but until lately I

was sure I was stronger than you and that you would do everything I wanted you to do.'

'Not on your life,' said David with spontaneous energy.
'I've been talking like a prig, but that was because I was
hunting for the right words, and couldn't find them; but I
wouldn't let you rule me, any more than I would attempt to
rule you. For both our sakes I've got to get my own way in a
few important things; marriage for instance.'

'Yes – well, I've given way about that.'

'Of course you have, and it will be as soon as I can get a
special licence. Mercifully that doesn't take long. After that –
well, I don't delude myself I can make you happy within a few
days, but in time I shall; not because I'm strong or noble or
even clever, but because we're meant to make a success of our
future.'

The moonlight had dimmed, and there was a faint hint
of dawn in the sky. Pearl looked up at it, as though she had
never seen the sky before. Half-silver and half-grey, eternity lay
beyond it and around them, and it belonged alike to the happy,
the heartbroken and those who propound wistful questions.
She said : 'I love you, darling. I shall never forget this hour.'

Pearl thought of many things as they drove through the cold
morning light, which presently was cold no longer, for the
sun replaced the moon and its first rays shone down upon
them.

The birds called to one another, sleepily at first and then
more imperatively; dew touched the grass with glistening
crystal, trees and hedges turned from grey to brilliant green,
tightly folded flowers began to unfurl their petals.

The future was blank no longer, but something of boundless
promise. She did not doubt that there would be sorrow and
pain and difficulties, but there would be happiness also, and
love would help them solve their problems.

She thought of her many friends whom she had neglected
since Cynthia's death; now they would also be David's friends.
She thought of Graham Bernard, but knew that because he
truly cared for her in his way, he would in time be glad for
her in her happiness and would do his best for her. She
thought of Kate, to whom she would write with affection,
and of Miles whom she still loved, whom she would always
love, and whom she would one day meet again. But by then

they would be on a different footing, and she would be a different Pearl.

Rose's charm was still in her suit pocket, and she fingered it from time to time, but presently when they were passing a stretch of water, a pond upon which a swan was swimming in pride and beauty, she took it out and showed it to David.

'What shall I do with this?' she asked. 'I told you how I found it.'

'Do you want to keep it?'

'Not now. It will remind me of too much unhappiness. I thought – perhaps, I'm not really superstitious, but I'd rather nobody else had it.'

David took the charm from her. He stopped driving, and threw it far into the pond. Glancingly, it struck the swan on the head, and the creature looked at them with such indignant rebuke that they both laughed.

The charm was so light and small, that it made not the slightest ripple as it sank, and David said : 'I'm not exactly superstitious, but I'm glad it's gone.'

It was midday before they reached London, though they stopped on the way only once, and that was at a wayside café. Even then Pearl did not leave the car, but David brought out coffee and buttered rolls and coaxed her to eat and drink. Exhausted though she was Pearl was happy, and not with exultant excitement, but with peace and trust and hope.

'The house has been empty for months, but I think poor old Amy will be there, and will have straightened things up as much as she can,' said Pearl, as they drove through the London suburbs. 'I wrote to her a week ago, when I knew we should be coming here, and sent her the keys. She was Aunt Cynthia's maid for years, but when Aunt Cynthia was very ill Amy fussed so she got on her nerves, and I was unkind – and dismissed her.'

'But could you help it, if she upset your aunt?'

'I could have done it differently, or I could have kept Amy out of the sick room, but I was worried and miserable, and I didn't care if Amy suffered. She came to the funeral though, and I did say then that I was sorry, and last week, when I wrote, I told her if she liked to come back to me, she could fuss and I wouldn't get impatient with her.'

David, though he thought that might be a difficult promise

to keep, pressed her hand and said : 'It was sweet of you.'

'Well, it wasn't so sweet really. It was only Aunt Cynthia who hated being fussed over, I rather liked it.'

To David, when the elderly maid opened the door to them, there was pathos in the radiance which lit up the lined face. Pearl gave her her hand, and the old woman clung to it as she stammered out words of greeting.

She was more happy than she could say to welcome her dear Miss Pearl again; her bedroom was ready for her, and so was one for the gentleman friend she had written would be staying with her.

David thought there was painful doubt in the glance the old woman turned upon him, and he said : 'Only a friend for a few days, I hope. Miss Pearl and I are getting married, Amy, and you must come to our wedding.'

Evidently this was the best of all possible news. It was what Miss Cynthia had hoped for, said Amy. She had always said Miss Pearl needed someone to take care of her.

This and more was chattered at them as Amy opened the door of the dining-room. She would be no time getting them sleep. Worn out, she must be, travelling all through the night. a meal, she promised, and then Miss Pearl must have a long

When they were left alone, Pearl said : 'We can leave everything to her as you see. It will have to be a church wedding to satisfy her, with Aunt Cynthia s friends invited – at very short notice I fear – to be present, and what Amy will describe as a *reshershy* reception afterwards ! She will even fix me a dress. I left several here, and Amy is good at altering and reviving.'

'Do you mind?'

'Not now. I'd like people to meet you and think how lucky I am and to wish us good fortune.'

Pale and strained though her face was, David saw in it a promise of the happy girl she would be one day. He said : 'I'm not good enough, but . . .'

How could he say that, she wondered, after all she had told him about herself. But he meant it. He would always mean what he said to her.

'This is our home,' she said softly, 'it belongs to us both, and may we be happy here, and always keep our love alive.'